Time and Robbery

Time and Robbery

by

Rebecca Ore

Aqueduct Press

Seattle

Aqueduct Press, PO Box 95787
Seattle, WA 98145-2787
www.aqueductpress.com

ISBN: 978-1-933500-87-4
First printing, March 2012

Library of Congress Control Number: 2011941633

10 9 8 7 6 5 4 3 2 1

Cover Design by Lynne Jenson Lampe

Grunge Tree Man: ©istockphoto.com/John Woodcock
Sleepy Rural (Barns): ©istockphoto.com/Andvari Images
Glacier: Pfeffer, W.T. 2004. Columbia Glacier: From the Glacier
Photograph Collection. Boulder, Colorado USA: National Snow and
Ice Data Center/World Data Center for Glaciology. Digital media.

Book Design by Kathryn Wilham

For those who wear true masks.

Joseph Tavistock first saw Isobel fishing, wading in a chalk stream, blue hippie dress floating around her knees. Her dark tumbled hair glinted in the light, the stream bouncing spangles against her chin. She cast to rising trout, caught and released one. Tavistock said, "Are you teasing trout?"

Her eyes locked onto Tavistock's, but she didn't answer for what felt like minutes. Tavistock twitched in the silence until she finally said, "Educating them." After she waded out of the stream with her long skirt wetly wrapped around her legs, Tavistock got her mobile number. The first night they were together, her orgasm pulled the condom off his cock. They moved in together a few years before Tavistock got the job. The Job; he thought of it in capital letters.

Joseph Tavistock's London was the Empire imploded. Sikhs in turbans talking Cockney took bus fares. Huge percentages of the world's population appeared to want to be in London, legally or not. His London was also the anonymous chrome-ribbed office flats and attached houses with Miami art deco effects, built as speculative projects for bank clerical staff and now used by Ministry of Defense subcontractors.

He fell in love with The Job when two armed guards took him to the server room that he'd never see again, but would connect to for half his working life. The cages, woven of wire thick enough to hold wolves, were recycled from internet companies gone bankrupt in 2002. The cabinets looked slightly newer. Lights glowed—blue, red, amber, white—in the chilled air. The machines in the cages and lockers were purpose-built for security and ran operating systems adapted for these machines: not precisely Linux, nor Windows, nor Mac OS. The networks they connected to were encrypted and ran on dedicated fiber-optic cables. *The toys, the toys*, Tavistock thought as he walked through the data center, *a whole new operating system, a network with no downtime.*

Other people's toys built the challenges. Most of the illegal immigrants came in by airplane with impeccable passports produced by various Karachi and Beijing operations in offices that resembled his own.

After work, Tavistock had Isobel.

When Tavistock went through clearance for The Job, Isobel told Tavistock she was the child of Welsh hippies, born in a commune, without any record of birth at the time, home-schooled—not much proof of a life before she was 16. They had to establish that people knew the commune, knew her parents, and saw her grow up, that she was British.

"That's the last I want to hear from your job," she'd said after the clearance came through. Tavistock loved his wife with great beauty and no curiosity about his work. Isobel was his escape from the side of the job that wasn't play on the machines: interviewing people who were either liars or frightened, examining passports for what could be time's damages or could be signs of modern forgeries, writing reports on people he'd interviewed whose passport chips malfunctioned. The interrogations were the other duties as assigned his masters didn't explain in the technical interviews and which looked like an afterthought in his contract.

His wife, trained in commune life, could cook, make cheese and butter, spin, weave, and sew, and had a box of erotic devices. When she moved in with him, she had brought in a grand piano, worth around £4,000 and older than she was, that filled the dining room. Tavistock didn't ask how she'd gotten it. He'd been with her when she gave birth to their son, cut the cord, and gave it to her to keep safe in some ritual way she must have learned on the commune.

The government tempted him with the machines, but then trained him in the laws around arrests and even gave him a warrant card, turning him half cop. To make up for the stale interviews in airport back rooms, a year into The Job, Tavistock wrote a program scanning passports for anomalies that would show up in multi-decade scans of recorded passports. His program ran on the caged secure servers miles away.

After running five minutes, his program found a pattern that he hadn't expected: a series of men coming from France, born there of British mothers, all the mothers apparently connected to a house in Somerset, spread out over a century. The men and their mothers had turned up at the British consulate when the men were 18 or so, claiming passports as their rights as British citizens born on foreign soil. The fathers were unknown, probably Arabs or gypsies, since all the men were relatively darker skinned than British pale.

Tavistock called up the scanned-in photographs from the passports. The earliest ones hadn't had the photographs recorded, but the last two men looked like twins except for slight padding in the gums that made the lips and cheeks look something different: not actual differences in facial construction—broad heads that were lighter along the lower face without being weak. He stared at the last photograph and called up the travel records for the man. Strange middle name, Velius. First name was William. Surnamed Parker.

Parker was now living on a farm in Slovakia, raising DNA-reconstructed mammoths. Tavistock knew that these very official passports were based on lies. He guessed that the women had been smuggling in Eurasians, and the present man had gone home or close to it. Not necessarily his problem unless the man came back to the UK on that fake passport. People with forged passports in the UK now were the problems Tavistock was paid to investigate, not some eccentric raising mammoths in Eastern Europe.

The next week, he received an email from a cyber-café in Bratislava with a link to a site that had a video waiting for him. The email had said, "I may need your help. Look at this. Velius." He downloaded the video onto a laptop he could wipe easily if the video was wormy or virus infected. It was a strange video, no sound, camera apparently fixed in position—no panning, digital zooms, choppy editing. The landscape was nothing Tavistock was familiar with, though the hills looked vaguely Scottish or Norwegian. Only the climate was wrong, dry and cold, and the plants were wrong.

The video had the flavor of amateur porn shot through a window, but seemed both more real and more unreal. A younger version of the last photograph of the last passport holder, a scrawny boy with long legs, apparently wounded but healing, was being raped. Another man attempted to stop the rapist, but didn't try that hard. A group of women and children huddled together, watching with various expressions: horror, resignation, boredom, or disassociation. The video jumped to a scene taken a bit later, with the young male lying on his back, eating dried meat that one of the women brought him, slipping it to him with her body blocking anyone seeing what she was doing. She looked back over her shoulder. They talked briefly when he finished eating. She gave him something from a skin bottle. She went off camera and came back with the man who'd tried to stop the rape. The young male spoke, eyes almost unblinking as if he could get the man to hear better if he fixed the man with his eyes. The man shook his head, a gesture that seemed jarringly contemporary.

The next scene was of someone holding a flint knife, talking over the boy and a very young girl, maybe two years old, both lying on their bellies.

The last shot was of the boy sitting on a log staring at the camera.

For a cold second, Tavistock wondered if he'd been framed for child pornography and decided not to show anyone else the video. He asked himself again what was the landscape and decided to see what he could find out about the man in the landscape and the contemporary passport photograph.

He wondered if he could get fingerprints and check them against world criminal records.

✹

The team met in an office that was behind two locked doors in a building they shared with a Farsi television station and an avionics firm with other government contracts. The building was a long two-story modern thing outside London proper. Tavistock's team had a contract with the Home Office to improve detection of illegals. They budgeted for a large coffee urn, a supply of pastries that different team members brought in from different shops, varying that as much as possible. They shredded their garbage because the US had reported that foreign agents deduced advance knowledge of one of their operations from the late night pizza deliveries in the morning trash.

The team all, even the women, wore jeans and assorted vendor tee-shirts and, depending on weather and mood, decorative or functional boots and shoes. Tavistock suspected that their counter-parts all over the world as well as their adversaries wore the same jeans and tee-shirts, with shoes varying by climate.

Marcus Jones was already seated, sipping coffee and reading a copy of the *Guardian*, muttering under his breath at the articles. Part Welsh but claiming more, and quietly gay, Marcus was Tavistock's oldest teammate, the one who could be counted on to be judiciously mistrustful without being paranoid. After Tavistock sat down by Marcus, Simon Burns came in with the pastries of the day and put them on the credenza to the side of the conference table. Burns was the junior male, Oxford degree in the Moderns, self-trained in programming. He dropped technical terms—arrays, sorts—but had more a reading knowledge of Perl than any ability to program. He was lean with dark hair a bit too long, ambitious to move into a position he could brag about, not really a technical boy.

Lisa McPherson and Dora Gray came in together, talking about some BBC show they'd both seen last night about remains of Vikings, who had been captured and slaughtered by the Saxons. As they sat down at their places at the table, Dora said, of the massacre, "What a waste of cock." They were the women on the team. Dora Gray handled biometrics and DNA analysis; Lisa kept the minutes of the meeting. Tavistock's team reported to Peter Cooper, who took reports from all the intrusion teams and sent them on to the appropriate officials. He was the project manager for the contract and a government employee on the client side. Today, as typical when nothing needed client interactions, he wasn't in the office. He managed more contracts than just Tavistock's team's.

Tavistock said, "My program found an anomaly in about five minutes. Some family in Somerset has been getting passports for men claiming to be the natural sons of family women who lived in France. Been going on since maybe the late nineteenth century. I've been doing some follow-up."

Simon asked, "How many?"

"Looks like six, all between 16 and 18 when they applied for a passport."

Dora said, "Well, not in bulk, then. Where do they go after they get the passports?"

"Apparently, they're joining a family antique business, only it's passed through the women and not the men. The main shop is in London." Tavistock didn't mention the strange video. "House in Somerset. They make periodic buying trips in the EU."

"Smuggling, you think?" Simon said.

"I really don't know."

"What's the latest guy's name?"

"William Velius Parker."

"Odd middle name," Dora said. "Check up on it, but don't put too much time into it. It's just one guy, and we've got worse problems."

Lisa scribbled but didn't say anything. Simon Burns leaned back from the conference table and said, "We've got several obvious cases of forged birth certificates, with people claiming to be eligible to return to the UK as grandchildren of immigrants. The forger is in Karachi, so we don't know what this is about."

They want to live somewhere stable where they can set up takeaway shops, Tavistock thought but didn't say. He thought about his own kin, a handful scattered between various housing estates and lower-middle-class outer suburbs, not people he'd miss if the world economy went topsy turvey and Karachi had better opportunities.

Tavistock emailed back to the man who'd sent him the video. "Received your video. Not really to my taste. Where did it take place?"

The reply was several days later. "Scotland, I think."

Pretty non-committal, Tavistock thought. He sent another message, "Too many men have been born in France to women from a family in Somerset. And they all went into the antique business the women's sisters or cousins owned."

The reply was instant. "Who knows?"

Tavistock ignored the email. He did a public records search and found out that William Velius Parker had been in a civil union with a police investigator who subsequently left him. Exes could be useful. He took a day to drive to Somerset, glad he lived south of London. He drove by the house where Parker had lived when he was last in England. The main house was an old traditional hall, with a newer two-story tower, wider than a defense tower, with even wider space on the ground level. A chimney ran up one side of the tower. Around the house were low barns, looking almost prehistoric. Tavistock wondered if anyone would show him around if he asked, decided not to. He stopped at a small shop in the crossroads and asked about the man who had lived in the house, showed a passport photograph. The shopkeeper had been drinking a bit, a wet but empty glass by the cash register. "Ah, yes, Vel, he's luck for all of us in this part of Somerset."

"How long was he living here?"

The man acted as though that was a trick question, and said, "Are you getting petrol or lunch?"

"I'm looking for the man who used to be his partner."

"Thomas, he's with someone else now, you know. Why are you asking?"

"Want to talk to him about getting antiques." Not absolutely a lie.

"Family's shop is in London. Vel comes back from time to time to pull things out of storage. Go see them."

When Tavistock found Thomas, the old man was unhelpful in the way that a trained officer can be so very unhelpful without appearing to be hiding anything. He said that he didn't hold anything against Vel and still had warm feelings for him, but hadn't kept in touch. Tavistock wondered if he'd email Vel a warning that a man had been in his neighborhood asking questions.

The old paper public records for Somerset had some curious gaps, as though someone had edited things out over the centuries. In one fifteenth-century court record book, the bottom of a page had been torn out. Tavistock wished even harder for fingerprints. He wondered if he could make an excuse for wandering into the low barns by the house.

It's not the house itself, and I was taking shelter from the weather, he decided to claim if anyone found him there. He went into the first barn and came to a double door that looked like an air lock. Smuggling? He tried to see if the lock was pick-able with anything he had in his pockets. A credit card popped it back. He expected alarms or a dog and man to come bursting in on him.

He walked into a museum of relics from the Paleolithic and Neolithic, things that looked like they'd never been in the ground. He'd never heard of a private collection like this, but surely scholars knew of it.

A girl with dyed green hair stood up from behind one of the counters. She looked terrifying at first, almost supernatural considering the hair and her old woman's eyes in the prepubescent face, body with the very beginning buds of breasts. He calmed down slightly when he realized her age, still scared since he was breaking and entering. They stood looking at each other without speaking for what seemed like a minute or more. Tavistock wondered if she had herself broken in.

"I knew you'd be here," she said. "I'm Quince. You'll need physical evidence to keep from looking crazy." She opened the case in front of her and pulled out a Neolithic pot, polished but not glazed. He saw finger impressions in the clay around the base, as though someone had held it before firing it. "Take it," she said. When he did, her fingers brushed his, and he felt tremendously uneasy, as though she'd put that uneasiness into him with her touch.

"Who are you?"

"Vel's daughter by sperm donation. Don't worry, I won't tell anyone you broke in. He wants to cooperate with you, but the whole story might seem rather insane. The real trick is whether you'll cooperate with him. He can be flighty. And he can be really melodramatic at times."

Tavistock recognized the assumed adult tone of a child almost adolescent gossiping about family and relaxed. He smiled at her. "Don't you think the barn needs to be better locked up?"

"Vel will put on better locks now that you've got the pot," Quince said. She stood where she was as he turned to walk out with the pot. He looked back when he got to the door. She was still standing behind the case the pot came from. She smiled slightly back at him, but he was too far away to see if the eyes still looked so very old.

Tavistock found Quince's birth record, father an anonymous sperm donor and mother Carolyn Parker, another family member with a failed relationship, formerly in a domestic partnership with a woman anthropologist. He decided to call the former partner from the road as he went home.

That one talked but only knew that the family celebrated Yule in a unique way that she wanted to study further, but Vel had stopped inviting her back after one Yule ceremony.

"Does everyone call him Vel?"

"Oh, yes. I think it's a family name. The family seemed to have been a refuge for gay kids from the time of Henry the Eighth on. Always some gay man who rescued the boys and gave them beards among the young women. Family appears to be about a third gay. One of the kids said the house at Yule was like a sexual Brigadoon, a place where everyone was accepted."

He got a partial print off the pot and tried to see if anything matched it. The only near match was an arrest for solicitation in Atlanta, Georgia, in 1951. He requested any photographs they might have.

The mug shots showed the young boy from the video. Healthier looking, though, Tavistock thought. 1951? The current holder of the passport didn't look to be over 30.

So one man had been getting multiple passports, to disguise how long he'd lived. Tavistock didn't know if he could take this to his team yet without seeming crazy. He asked Dora to do a dating on the pot without explaining why. She would do it without asking more questions.

He went back to Somerset to see if he could find Quince at the house, but her mother, Carolyn, answered the door. The woman was lighter skinned than the people in the video but could otherwise have been the man's sister. When he introduced himself, she stiffened. Her face relaxed fractionally to let her lips move to tell him that Quince wasn't available. He knew that Carolyn had been Vel's physician, and records indicated that she'd brought him back from Amsterdam in a privately chartered helicopter a short time before his lover left him.

Lots of information, Tavistock thought, behind that rigid face.

In bits of old Somerset records and in one London record, he'd found odd mentions of a man with a mutilated little finger on the left hand. This matched the boy in Atlanta, but the current man didn't have a mutilated little finger.

Tavistock suspected he'd sound crazy now that the missing fingertip was no longer missing, but he wanted to have someone else notice and tell him the non-missing fingertip meant different people before he dropped the case. He missed pure work on the machines—not this chasing people face-to-face over ambiguous passports.

"Okay, let me try this on you all. We've got someone who seems to have lived longer than most humans, getting help with passports, apparently from women in his family, if it is his family. He sells antiques. Some of his clients are connected, a few Royals."

Dora said, "The pot dates about 5,000 years before present, if that has any connection to this. The prints are sort of problematic, but I suspect that you could get something from them. Did you try?"

"Came up with a 1951 arrest for solicitation in Atlanta, Georgia. The kid didn't speak English, didn't have papers on him, and nobody else in the raid knew who he was or what nationality. Marks, minus his little finger tip on his left hand, cut just below the nail bed, middle of the joint, apparently. He disappeared. Out of the cell, apparently. They didn't have television monitoring then, so they assumed the other prisoners who said he just disappeared were lying." Tavistock passed the photographs of the boy arrested in 1951 in Atlanta and of the current passport holder.

Marcus said, "What better antique dealer than someone who knows the goods from manufacture on?"

Simon said, "Or we're being hoaxed by someone, maybe the Americans for some reason. Or you're nuts, Joseph."

Dora asked, "Do you have DNA samples for the family and for the man?"

"He's out of the country at the present."

"You might want to drop this one," Marcus said. "What do we do with him if we catch him, if he's been alive for so long? If those are his fingerprints on the pot, then he's had excellent luck for several thousand years. Or he can't be killed. Or we're all going to get committed to hospital for bringing this to anyone's attention. Or someone's testing our defenses with a hoax."

Simon said, "I don't think we should drop it at all. If this is a hoax, Cooper needs to hear about it. We're keeping this from our project manager—how's this going to look if Cooper finds out from someone else that the team didn't report a hoax."

Marcus tightened his lips and looked at Tavistock. "Joe doesn't pull things like that."

Simon said, "Think about the...."

"...advantages to your career?" Lisa said. Tavistock noticed that she had stopped taking notes.

"If he's just a one-off, then it can be handled by ignoring the situation as long as he's in Eastern Europe, "Marcus said. "I don't want to have to explain the magical child with the Neolithic pot or breaking in to the man's private museum to our superiors."

"Simon, would you want to be the one who tells Cooper about this?"

"Think on it," Dora said.

Lisa said, "It just sounds too crazy. Someone's conning us. Let's leave it. If the man comes back to the UK, we can talk to him."

Simon muttered about the difference between the improbable and the impossible.

After the meeting was over, Dora came up to Tavistock and said, "The pot is Neolithic. If the prints are in the glaze or clay, it's a hard hoax to set up. There is something about his mammoths. Most of them aren't from the known reconstructed DNA lines. I found this curious when I first heard about it from the mammoth re-constructors. Nobody looked at the source too closely as it's terrible convenient in avoiding inbreeding depression. Mammoths turn out to be highly fussy and delicate beasties, prone to all sorts of elephant diseases."

Time travel? Long-lived? Both together felt like cheating. Tavistock set up a program to scan for uses of either Vel's National Health Card or his passport.

He got email a week later. The system flagged use of Vel's National Health Card. Vel had stumbled from a toilet stall to the emergency room lobby at a trauma intake hospital in South London, bleeding from a gunshot wound. *Poor bastard, gotcha.* Tavistock pulled out his work laptop and drove to the hospital.

✳

The family lawyer and Carolyn were already there. Carolyn recognized him, and her face froze again before she said, "This is Vel's attorney. Direct all your questions to him." Tavistock nodded but didn't speak. He opened his laptop to see when Vel had come back to the UK. The records he could access located Vel in Slovakia as of two hours earlier. Impossible moved to improbable.

He walked away from Carolyn and the lawyer and texted Marcus to say that they couldn't ignore Vel now, to prepare paperwork for holding him as a passport violator. Time and space violator, too. Marcus got the legal work done very quickly, then faxed the warrant and authorization to act in an official capacity back. Tavistock looked at the paperwork and closed the laptop, fingers tingling. He looked over at Carolyn and the lawyer huddled together, and felt slightly guilty, then annoyed at them for being there.

Tavistock showed his warrant card to the circulating nurse and said that he needed to see William Velius Parker.

"He's already got a Metropolitan policeman with him."

"This is a terrorist suspect," Tavistock said, exaggerating. The nurse showed him into the emergency surgical prep area.

Vel was lying on a gurney, shaved down the belly for surgery. Two orderlies were searching him for additional bullet entry points and running an ultrasound probe over his body. Heat lamps had them sweating in their coveralls as their glove-clad fingers moved down Vel's spine, lifting each arm to check the axilla, moving his legs apart to check the folds of the buttocks and groin.

He appeared to be an older version of the boy in the video, fuller bodied, still with the runner's legs, hairy now. Two IV lines ran into his arms with whole blood hanging above one and a clear liquid coming down another. A catheter and blood pressure gauge came out from between his legs. Webbed with tubing, Tavistock thought. The duty nurse looked at Tavistock and moved her hand toward the oxygen mask.

Vel wasn't screaming as the orderlies moved his legs and arms, which suggested they'd already given him some heavy painkillers. Tavistock doubted he could talk now. Probably he wouldn't remember anything.

The lawyer came in and said, "You do understand that he has had some delusions."

"He managed to get to this hospital without registering on any of the airport or Chunnel check points. Private plane?"

"Metropolitan police are already investigating the shooting. The family is working with them on this, and I will encourage Vel to cooperate fully with the Metropolitan police."

Tavistock said, "Vel's passport is not in order."

"You're the man who's been asking questions near his family home."

"Yes, and I'm with National Border Security."

The surgical nurse interrupted. "We're taking him in to surgery. His doctor explained about the special needs, liver sensitivity to antibiotics, lactose intolerance, and some possible mental issues. You both can see him when he wakes up."

"What are his chances?" Tavistock asked.

The nurse said, "Pretty good since he was shot in the emergency room toilet and managed to get to the lobby within minutes of that. We're going to open him up and patch the bowel and close any damaged blood vessels. The vascular surgeon is on her way. We've got a general abdominal surgeon scrubbed and ready to open him up."

Tavistock wanted to go in with them, but they only allowed the Metropolitan uniformed officer in. Tavistock and Vel's lawyer followed an orderly to the surgical waiting room. Carolyn was already there, talking with the circulating nurse.

Tavistock asked, "Did he say who did this?"

"No," the lawyer said. "At least not to me. I don't know what he told the officer."

"A month ago, he asked me to help him. I had been checking the family history of your women having children in foreign countries with those children, all male, showing up at 18 or so for British passports."

The lawyer said. "Our women have had children by strangers in various countries. We're not a traditional family."

"Why would he ask you to help him?" Carolyn said.

"I have no idea."

The circulating nurse came in and said that the vascular surgeon had started repairing the blood vessels. After that the general surgeon would repair the bowel. They'd found an artifact along Vel's pelvis bone that they'd turned over to the Metropolitan policeman since on ultrasound, the nodule—calcium and fibrous tissue—looked like it contained a stone arrowhead.

Tavistock opened his laptop and put in a requisition for the calcium nodule that contained the arrowhead. He also got the name and badge number of the officer with Vel. He texted Marcus to bring a fingerprint kit, then felt he'd forgotten something. His fingertips tingled. He shook his hands and balled them into fists to get rid of the feeling.

"So, why are you here?" Carolyn asked.

"Your daughter Quince gave me a Neolithic pot. Closest fingerprint match I got was for a 1951 US solicitation bust. Atlanta, Georgia. No papers, no English, and he disappeared. Mug shots look like the man with the current passport, only younger. I don't know why he said he might need my help or why your daughter made my job easier." Carolyn and the lawyer looked at each other, then at the floor. Tavistock began to worry that he'd said too much too soon. He asked, "Do you have any idea why he was shot?"

"No idea. Isn't Slovakia an EU country now? There aren't any border checks for EU countries," Carolyn said.

Tavistock didn't mention the video. Marcus came in to drop off the fingerprint kit and a printed warrant for Vel's arrest on a charge of passport irregularities. The most irregular thing was his not using it to come back to the UK. Tavistock watched Marcus go out. He didn't show the lawyer what he had yet.

"You must understand that Vel...William has episodes of mania. Once he's out of danger from the surgery, we'd like to get him into a facility," the lawyer said.

"Someone shot him. That should worry you much more than it seems to."

The lawyer said, "Vel said that person won't be back."

That's what I forgot. Tavistock texted Marcus's phone to see if he could bring over the tests for gunpowder residue on Vel's hands. Carolyn began pacing the floor. Marcus responded, "Check bag." The test kit for gunpowder residue was in the bag with the fingerprint kit. "Thinking ahead good," Tavistock texted back. He looked at Carolyn and felt slightly guilty for enjoying the puzzle.

Tavistock went to the bathroom stall where the blood trail ended to see if he could find any weapons. The toilet was marked closed, but Tavistock pulled out his identification and went on in. A Scene of Crime Officer was going through the waste bins. He'd finished photographing the scene, he told Tavistock. He had fingerprints from the stall door handle. Tavistock asked him to pass those on.

"No blood spatters, and he has an exit wound. Just blood on the floor. No weapons. Only one pair of bloody foot prints, his, I assume."

"Could he have been lying down?"

"No exit bullet, either. If he'd been lying down, the bullet would be on the floor and would have chipped the tiles."

"Nobody could have brought him in here?"

"We're checking the CCTV cameras, but all we've got so far is him coming out of the toilet into the lobby. Good place to get shot, in the toilet off the emergency room lobby, I suppose. How the shooter got out, I can't figure. Maybe swung out over the blood pool from the top of the toilet..."

"Could someone have tampered with the CCTV cameras?" Tavistock knew the answer was yes, of course.

"Only way in is through the lobby. Someone would have seen folks lugging a shot man in."

Tavistock found out that Marcus had already asked for all records on the case to be sealed and went to the waiting room to sit until this strange character woke up.

He didn't say more to the family lawyer or Carolyn, the family doctor, just asked the circulating nurse where he could get coffee. He carried his bag and laptop with him to get the coffee, horrible vending machine stuff, called Isobel to say he'd be late getting home, urgent case, and then went back to the waiting room and played solitaire on his laptop until the circulating nurse said that Vel was in recovery and beginning to show signs of consciousness.

The Metropolitan officer was in the recovery room. "Word's come down that you and yours will be taking over," he said. "He says he doesn't know who shot him. I'll be leaving it in your hands." As he stood to leave, he straightened out his uniform, making Tavistock suddenly aware of his jeans and vendor tee-shirt.

The recovery room nurses didn't want all three of them by the bed. Tavistock looked at the lawyer and said, "I think we should all be here for this."

Carolyn took Vel's nearest hand, watching out for the IV needle in his inner elbow and the oxygen monitor on his index finger. The head of his bed was elevated, and he had an oxygen tube with the double ends in his nostrils. He was covered from his collarbones to his feet with a white sheet. Two tubes ran out under the lower end of the sheet. Tavistock stood watching, his laptop and kit under his left arm.

Vel's eyelids fluttered. He opened his eyes, but closed them again. "Carolyn," he said. Tavistock wished he'd taken the prints earlier while Vel was still unconscious. The man seemed to be in considerable pain. The usual repair surgery for abdominal gunshot was to open the patient from just below the sternum to just above the pelvic bone and see what the damage had been.

The surgeon came in and said, "I doubt you remember what I explained before surgery, and so I'll tell you what we did. We opened you up and found a bruised kidney, which we're treating conservatively, two major blood vessels that needed repair, and a bisected colon, which I've repaired. You'll be in surgical recovery until you look stable, then we'll move you to surgical intensive care for at least the night. Then I believe this gentleman has some questions for you." The surgeon nodded at Tavistock.

I'm not really a cop. I'm not really enjoying this part, taking fingerprints in front of the family. Tavistock tried to bring back his earlier pleasure in having found his man. He said, "I'm Joseph Tavistock. We have a warrant for your arrest on suspicion of passport fraud and possible smuggling. I'll take your fingerprints as gently as I can, and then I'm going to do a test for gunpowder residue."

"Joe Tavistock," Vel said. He closed his eyes while Tavistock took the prints and pushed the wax strips against Vel's palms. One of the nurses took the oxygen monitor off so he could test Vel's index finger on the dominant hand.

The lawyer said, "My client—"

Vel opened his eyes and said, "—he knows."

The lawyer said, "Like I said, episodes of mania."

Vel moved his eyes toward the lawyer and said, "No, he needs to help me."

Why me, Tavistock thought. Nobody said anything more. Vel began weeping silently, not sobbing. The nurses ran everyone out except for Carolyn, who sat down beside him and stroked his shoulder as they left. Tavistock called for someone else who was cleared to come in and spend the rest of the night watching while they arranged for a cleared medical team to take over Vel's care in the hospital. His service could use one of the locked private rooms on the top floor. He went out into the hall with the lawyer.

The lawyer said, "I'm going to ask you to prove the passport irregularities in court."

Tavistock said, "That would be a seriously bad idea for both sides. What is he? What is he to you? Bunch of women have been helping him get British passports since Victoria's time. And we're going to pull the Official Secrets Act down on him and everyone who has been aiding and abetting him." Tavistock thought about the video, of the women with Vel, the tribe that was fucking Vel and the women.

The lawyer said, "We'll talk to the Home Office about this. Vel has friends."

"I'd suggest that you not do that."

Tavistock went home when his relief arrived. He would give Dora the nodule the surgeon took out of Vel's pelvis in the morning. At midnight, the relief man called to ask if Vel's Eastern European lover could sit with Vel so Carolyn could rest. Tavistock said, "Check his passport and if he flew in legally, let him in but watch him. Record what they say."

Carolyn came by his house at about 1 a.m. Isobel let her in. Tavistock was trying to sleep, but got dressed to see her. He had no idea how she'd found his house; he supposed the agency had a bad security leak of its own. They went into his home office.

Carolyn said, "Vel wants something from you. I have no idea what it is. I don't know why he didn't get us to arrange something where he couldn't be disappeared and dissected. We're his family. We could have helped him, whatever it is."

"We can keep it quieter."

"He's kept us together for 14,000 years. Then he fucked off to Eastern Europe—but now, you know at least some of this. He's been our luck for thousands of years. And we've kept his secret for hundreds. This really doesn't seem like a good time for him to give himself up to the authorities. I worry about his mental health, really."

"He was shot in London. Aren't you concerned about someone coming back to try to kill him?"

When she didn't answer, Tavistock didn't say anything more. He sat watching her. The women in the video had a family feel to them. The women weren't standing up for him very much in that past, if the whole thing wasn't a reenactment. Tavistock finally said, "Your luck?"

"We've always had food. We escaped the worst of wars. We made the right political decisions. Thanks to Vel."

"Your luck, the poor bastard."

Isobel was playing softly on a recorder when he saw Carolyn out. She pulled the recorder out of her lips and said, "I won't ask."

"Thanks," Tavistock said. "Sorry it followed me home. I must have done something stupid." Tavistock wanted to sleep himself into a clearer head than the one he had now, but he had to finish the night's work.

She rolled her eyes at him as she put the recorder back in her mouth and kept playing.

Tavistock went into his home office to write up the visit, which he coded for his team only. He vibrated from fatigue while the room light sank into pre-sleep green. The team would have to tell Peter Cooper something to get time budgeted to the case. He checked his email before going back to bed. Quince had also come in, but the nurses sent her home. Too much for a young girl, but letting the lover in seemed like a good idea. And these were cleared nurses. Oh, well, they'd be watching. He wondered why everyone trusted the lover being there.

He went to bed. As tired as he was, Isobel stroked some life into him, then drained him completely. Forget everything until morning comes, he thought as he fell asleep in her arms while she sang to him in Welsh.

The next morning, Tavistock parted the curtains around Vel's bed and found Vel, turned on his side under a blanket, moving his fingers through a man's hair. Both of them were a bit stubbly, and the man looked, seated, as though he was slightly shorter than Vel's six feet and chunkier, though not fat. The lover had fallen asleep in a chair pushed up against the hospital bed, his head against the mattress. Vel woke up a bit more and tried to smile at Tavistock.

Tavistock wondered how they'd gotten the Eastern European here so fast and if he knew what Vel was. "Social grooming?" he asked.

"Lice picking. It's an old habit." The fingers had looked more purposeful than affectionate stroking.

"Do you miss the past?"

"Not lice. Or fleas." He tried to straighten up in bed, and the charge nurse, one of the cleared ones, came to help him. His lover murmured a bit and continued sleeping.

"I'm a secure nurse," the woman said. "We're keeping this quiet."

Vel sounded as though he hurt and was trying to hide it, much as wounded social creatures do. If he wanted to lie to Tavistock and say that his family, to preserve their luck, forced him to accept the fake passports, Tavistock would have almost wanted to believe him. Vel's lover stirred and looked up at Tavistock as though trying to remember who Tavistock was. He sat up in the chair and said to Vel, "In the future, you can't complain about my serving in Doctors Without Frontiers."

Vel tried to laugh, but winced. "Do you staple people together? They stapled me together. Whole belly down."

The lover said, "You've had the standard surgery for abdominal gunshot. I could have done it myself. And they're going to be sensible about the food."

"Something's stuck up my cock, Emil."

They treated Tavistock as furniture.

Emil said, "Yep, and you've got a blood pressure monitor in your groin and an oxygen monitor on your index finger. And pain killers and antibiotics in your veins."

Vel said, "What happens next?"

His lover got up and looked at the monitors to the left of the head of the bed. "You looked like you'd had a relatively uneventful night, blood pressure up a bit, in a healthy way, when we sat you up for the broth. Temperature normal. They'll probably pull all that stuff after the doctor does the morning rounds."

Tavistock said, "Will the gunpowder residue tests come back negative or not?"

Vel said, "Not. Self-defense."

Emil ignored Tavistock as he must have ignored whatever political authorities had waited by the bedsides of his patients in Asia and Africa. Tavistock saw from watching them that Emil knew about Vel's differences from normal human mortals. Tavistock wondered how Emil dealt with knowing Vel would bury him—though now they looked to be the same age—if they stayed together that long. He said, "I'd like to talk to you, doctor."

Emil looked him in the eyes then, for the first time, and said, "My papers are in order."

Tavistock almost said Emil's papers weren't his concern, but decided to become furniture again. The abdominal surgeon came in, looking at the machines first, then at Vel. He threw back the blanket and sheet covering Vel. The charge nurse removed the bandage over the incision. The staples gleamed against Vel's belly from sternum to the top of the pubic bone. The entry and exist wounds were bandaged. The surgeon said, "Some privacy, please."

Tavistock shrugged and stayed put. The nurse said, "We can deal with this."

Emil stroked Vel's forehead while the nurse pulled the gauze off the wounds. The doctor said, "We'll debride the entrance and exit wounds in a few days. Then we'll let them heal from the inside out. You can learn to change the dressing yourself, or have a visiting nurse do it for you." He called on his mobile for a table in one-day surgery. "I see that you had some broth in the night. How did you tolerate that?"

Vel said, "Loved it. I'm hungry now."

"Let's wait until after we pull the blood pressure monitor and the catheter. The nurse can pull the catheter now. We'll take you to a day-surgery suite to pull the blood pressure monitor since it's in an artery. We'll close the artery. You'll be conscious, and you can have breakfast when we bring you back here."

Tavistock looked away as Vel gripped Emil's hand while the nurse did this. She said, "We'll get you breakfast after we make you more comfortable." She looked at Tavistock, then re-bandaged the stapled incision and replaced the loose wadding on the entry and exit wounds.

The doctor said, "You also have a bruised kidney. I don't know if you remember my telling you this when you came out from anesthesia. It's from the bullet's stretch cavity—the shock."

Vel said, "I know what a stretch cavity is." He looked at Tavistock, who tried not to react. Vel was a rather informed patient, wasn't he?

More orderlies, now cleared orderlies, came to take Vel to the day-surgery suite. They asked him if he could get over the gurney himself, with help, or if they needed to log roll him over. Vel grimaced and tried to move over to the stretcher with as little help as possible. Tavistock told Emil, "Go with him if you want," not that Tavistock believed he could have stopped Emil.

Emil said, "Quince is coming to sit with him during the day. I didn't have much sleep. I've seen the procedure before. I'm having trouble seeing all this happening to him."

"His daughter."

"Yes, his daughter, by his doctor. Is he under arrest?"

"I'd like to talk to you in private." Tavistock led Emil to a vending machine room that was empty. Emil sat down in one of the plastic chairs. Tavistock stayed on his feet.

Emil said, "I know about him."

Tavistock said, "I really wish you didn't." Tavistock looked at Emil for a long moment, trying to remember that he was supposed to be the one in charge here, but Emil didn't seem to take authority seriously. *Gay kid in Eastern Europe, probably not so interested in authority, what people thought.*

"I want to take him home, but he can't travel by air for at least six weeks."

"Couldn't he time-jump?" Tavistock wondered how Vel got in the toilet without signs of the bullet being in the toilet, too. A bit of a bluff question on his part. Tavistock wondered if he was too tired now to be effective as an interrogator. He preferred technical puzzles to human ones. He wasn't even an experienced interrogator.

Emil said, "You've got his family hostage."

"Yeah, his family. Anytime the crops failed, they could send him to the future to whore for groceries." Tavistock rocked on his feet a bit, thinking about how little he had to do with his own family, then tried to remember his two months of evening interrogator training.

Emil said, "He says they keep him sane."

"Last two centuries, he's been an antique dealer. I think at least some of his clients know."

"Vel is a very likeable man. My father likes him, despite everything." Emil looked at the door, then back at Tavistock.

Tavistock shrugged. Did Vel start playing him with the video when Vel realized he was investigating him? If the video showed real events in the past, then his family had traded his ass to someone nasty to join a stronger band. "Let's go back."

"Yes, that procedure doesn't take long unless they botch it," Emil said. He felt his chin and grimaced. "Need to shave." They went back to the recovery ward where the nurse showed them to Vel's bed and pulled the curtains around them.

Tavistock and Emil sat in the curtained off space looking at each other, then away as the orderlies brought

Vel back. Vel in that video looked quite a bit younger than this current Vel, no beard or body hair. Tavistock said, "My people have access to private rooms in this hospital, even a family dining room, on the top floor. More privacy than on a ward. We're not planning to put him on a prison ward."

Emil said, "He should be near an operating theater for the next few days. Then he could go to the house in Somerset. The family can post bail."

"We'll move him upstairs after he's stable. If anything happened, the Somerset house isn't close to a trauma center."

Vel seemed a bit groggy. He asked Emil, "How long can you stay?"

"A few days. I'm taking vacation time."

"Don't take all of it now. But I'm so glad you're here."

"He knows what I know." Emil jerked his head at Tavistock.

"Yes."

The nurse brought in a tray of low residue food: a quarter of boiled chicken breast, an egg, and something that looked like an anemic pudding. Vel let them raise the bed and pull over the bed table, holding his arms up to give them room to bring the table up. Then he ate, starting with the pudding, then the egg, finally the chicken.

"We'll up the pain med after you've eaten and get you on your feet," the nurse said. Vel looked at Emil as if checking to see if this was necessary. Emil nodded. Tavistock felt sleep deprived, but wanted to see Quince. He'd just learned that creatures like Vel existed. Now he wondered if Vel was the only one, but didn't think so. He suspected that the condition was genetic. His group would have to deal with all the bureaucratic concerns of dealing with something new whose powers and scope they didn't know yet. *At least, Vel isn't immune to bullets*, Tavistock thought. Solving the puzzle left him with the wounded man at the heart of the puzzle. He hoped working on the puzzle hadn't got Vel shot.

The nurse gave Vel additional pain meds, pulled the last IV needle out, and put him in a gown. When he was dressed and sitting on the edge of the bed, the nurse gave him a pillow to hold against the incision. He put it in place and nodded. Two orderlies helped him to his feet to walk. Emil pulled one away and took his place. Vel held onto Emil's shoulder with one arm while holding the pillow against his belly with the other. They made it the length of the ward. Vel was sweating a bit when he got back to his bed. "I'd like a shave," he said. Emil looked close to tears. Tavistock decided to see Quince later. His team was having a meeting on Vel at 10 a.m.

In the meeting, the group plus Cooper debated what to use Vel for, if they could use him, if the family was really sufficient hostage to get him to cooperate with them, and whether he was a unique mutation or one of a number of people like him who'd hidden from cultures who demonized them. Tavistock thought that perhaps they were looking at the reality behind the mythical gods, only Somerset had no myths that fit with Vel, just a silence. He said, "Vel had been their luck, not their master. Good neighbor, always opens the house up for a great party at Yule. Likeable man, apparently." Tavistock wondered how many centuries that had been going on.

Simon said, "His clients have been more talkative than his neighbors. 'Born in France, like his father and grandfather before him. Really knows his furniture makers.' The family has antiques, too, but they only sell them through Vel, of course. Nobody knows why he bought land in Slovakia, seem to think it had to do with his breakup with the old police detective."

Tavistock wondered if Vel knew about the future of DNA identification, of the assay on the calcium and tissue around the arrowhead. He didn't say that to the group, only, "I saw Vel at the hospital. He's doing about as well as can be expected after major abdominal surgery. They repaired him without a colostomy. He's eating already."

Cooper seemed both amused and irritated by the whole thing. He was from the same background as Simon, not from the technical side. "Props to whoever said he had to have powerful protectors to manage all this time." Simon nodded. "Some of his antique clients are asking about him. We're getting some pressure to treat him decently, whatever decently would mean in such a case."

"You're angry that we didn't tell you when we first suspected something," Marcus said.

"Nope, not talking about this made perfect sense until he came back, without passing customs, without time to have taken a train or plane from his last sighting in Slovakia, with gunpowder residue on his hand and all shot up. I'm still not convinced that he isn't crazy or that this isn't some practical joke from the Americans or someone else messing with us. How, by the way, does he explain the gunpowder residue?"

"Self defense," Tavistock said.

"Of course, and we have such proof," Cooper said drily. "When you take a man into custody, Joe, you're responsible for keeping him alive, so I want to know whether he has any more enemies who might want to kill him. I've got a budget line for this. Book time on SI 4567, and except for Joe, I don't expect more than a couple of hours a week on this. It's not going any further than my group of project managers at the present. I'm thinking about what to tell them."

"The family is matrilineal, which doesn't show up so easily in the Somerset marriage records but would work well with mitochondrial DNA tests. We'd like to do DNA tests on both him and the kin, if they are the kin and not some people who've been saying they're family for several centuries," Dora said. "I've got access to the Cambridge genome project equipment. I've done work for them and built up time owed on the machines there."

"Yes, if they've been forging passports for some stranger, it's a bit different than if they've been doing it for family. Do we have more or less leverage on him if they are or aren't his true family? We've got tissue samples from him, a section of the colon. Joe can get warrants for the family samples. Who'd have thought such a creature would have lawyers trying for disclosure? Okay, what can we use him for?"

Tavistock felt very tired then. "I think we need to look at the daughter. We know she was really born in England, when she was born, and have a DNA sample from her umbilical cord blood."

"Have you met her?"

"Yes. She gave up the pot with the fingerprints." Tavistock remembered that her touch had made him uneasy, that she touched the cleared orderly, and that everyone let Emil visit after she was at the hospital. What was the daughter? He didn't say anything to the group.

"She's thirteen. Maybe she's pissed at him for some reason," Cooper said. "Families don't always love each other."

Dora said, "He's her father, both of them said. They'll also share common mitochondrial DNA, a common mother. I've already tested that. Mitochondrial DNA will show what's what with the rest of the family. It's an easy test with modern equipment; take an afternoon for five samples. DNA paternity test, about the same level of difficulty, as I said, done and yes, he's the girl's father. Now how does he get the mammoth genes?"

"Apparently, he can jump in time," Tavistock said. "He said he didn't miss the past. But, he's nostalgic for mammoths."

Marcus said, "That's so cheating to have both longevity and the ability to time travel."

Cooper made some notes, then looked up and said, "Joe, we'll have people with him all the time, but we're going to let family members stay with him, too." He turned back to his notebook and jotted a few more notes. "It will all be under surveillance. We need some way to keep him from just fucking off to times he likes better. If he can really time travel. We have reason to believe long life. Time jumping simply is not as likely. What keeps him here now?"

"We've got his family as hostage," Tavistock said. "And maybe being in pain and drugged. I don't know."

Simon said, "Do you trust that? Someone put a bullet into him. Thousands of years ago, someone put an arrow into him. How do we control him? Maybe it would be better to let him die under anesthesia, take him apart, and see how he works."

"He looked human enough in the videos of the surgery," Dora said. "We've also got the ultrasound the hospital took before surgery."

Cooper shrugged and said, "Play hard and nice, kids, but don't neglect other work."

They all stood up and stretched a bit, then left the conference room. Joe and Dora ordered Carbon 14 tests on the material that had surrounded the arrowhead, which turned out to be a tiny quartz thing, still sharp, with a gold occlusion in the bulb of the projectile.

Back at the hospital, Tavistock found a woman, dark-haired, olive-skinned, bending over Vel, her fingers on his temples. Vel was looking up at her with dark liquid eyes, and Quince was standing far from the bed, against monitoring machines that hadn't been moved out yet, her face pale and her eyes very wide. Tavistock didn't recognize the woman from any files they'd been assembling on Vel's family. The nurse wasn't in the room.

The woman looked back at him as though he was only a transient nuisance. Quince held something in her hands that looked like a monitoring anklet. Vel murmured to the strange woman in a language Tavistock later found out was Greek, very old Greek. Tavistock asked, "Who are you?"

The woman said, "One of Vel's cousins."

"I'd like you to move away from the bed."

The woman and Vel exchanged an almost amused look, and the woman moved back. Quince's eyes followed the woman as she moved. The woman said, "I'm giving you a device from a time loop, so call it the Ouroboros Device. You need to feel like you have some control over him, and it will keep people like me from being able to pluck his brains out. Eventually, you'll open it up and figure out how to build it, and I'll bring the device you'll make back in time to now."

"Where's the nurse?"

Quince said, "I sent her out. It wasn't going to help to have her here. This is very bad."

Tavistock realized that this woman was the same kind of creature as Vel, unwounded, and nothing he could have done would have stopped her. He wasn't carrying a side arm.

Vel said, "You can go now, cousin."

"Good bye, Vel." And she stepped into invisibility. Later, they watched the tapes over and over, her stepping into invisibility.

Now, Tavistock turned to Quince and said, "I'd like to check that for fingerprints."

"She's not that stupid. She scared me."

Vel said, "She came to see if I was making a habit of killing the cousins."

Tavistock said, "And if she didn't like the answer, she'd have plucked your brains out? What does this device do? Should I believe either of you?"

"It keeps me from seeing probabilities, and it will keep me from jumping when I'm in better health. Can't jump when I'm injured this badly. Quince was going to bring the device to you. Diana wanted to beat Quince to me. The device works as advertised. I'd rather not have gone through surgery to have my brains plucked out by one of my own kind."

Quince said, "I don't know why she told such a stupid lie unless she thought we wouldn't cooperate with you." She came forward with the device.

Vel said, "Don't let her touch you. She's a contact telepath. Put it on the bed, Quince."

The nurse came back in then, looking a bit bewildered. Quince put the device on the bed, as sulky as any thirteen-year-old who didn't get her own way.

As Tavistock picked up the device, he said, "We're moving you upstairs now." He didn't know if the device worked or not, and was suspicious of what it really was, but needed to do something to feel like he'd done something. Vel looked at him and then at the device dangling in his fingers.

Quince said, "It locks shut and is tamper resistant. You can enter a numeric code when you lock it. Whoever puts it on can take it off, biometrics and code. It goes null state in five years, but your people will figure out how it works way before then, one way or another. Please put it on him."

"He's got to have more work done in three days," the nurse said.

"We can bring him back down for that, but I don't want him staying on an open ward." Tavistock remembered the woman stepping away to somewhere else, some other time. He'd like a large-scale version of the device he was putting on Vel's ankle, something that could wrap around a room, the whole of the UK. If the device really worked—Tavistock knew it could be some sham thing to lower their guard on Vel, but then how could they hold someone who could time-jump? And it was a shiny new machine to analyze. A machine to analyze was better than trying to figure out the motives of a man who had been living since the Stone Age and who could visit the future.

Vel said, "You need to feel like you can control me, and this is less nasty than being drugged or kept in pain."

The cleared orderlies came with a gurney. One said, "You should be able to help us. Otherwise, we'll have to log roll you again."

Vel scooted over onto the gurney, with the orderlies helping him a little. Quince watched, the corners of her eyes pinched in slightly.

"You hurt too much," she said.

"Sorry," Vel said as the orderlies straightened him out on the gurney. They wrapped a blanket over him. "One favor, Tavistock. Don't let them put me under for the debriding."

Quince said, "No general anesthesia. Please."

Tavistock said, "That's a medical decision, but I'll see what I can do."

The charge nurse said, "I'll note the request on his records. Vel, do you need more painkillers?"

"I'm good," Vel said. "Visitors? I need family."

"Yes," Tavistock said, "but they need to submit to a DNA test to prove they are family."

Quince walked by the stretcher. She bumped her hand against one of the orderlies' hand and looked back at Tavistock, her lips pulled tight. When Tavistock told the orderly, "Don't let her touch you again. She's a contact telepath," she struck out her tongue out at him

When they reached the private room, Vel said to Tavistock, "Quince can't jump. She can feel me and only me through the air."

Quince said, "Spoilsport."

Tavistock said, "Perhaps you'd be happier if you were a more normal child."

"I am not off the main sequence for being thirteen. I don't want to spend millennia in hiding." For a second she looked far older than thirteen and in pain. All Tavistock's work to quietly investigate her must have been screamingly obvious. Yet, she didn't run off. She said, "I will work for the Home Office when I turn fourteen. I'm going to be good for you, really."

Vel tried to turn in the new bed, gave up, and asked the orderlies to move him to his side and prop him with pillows so he wasn't lying on the entrance wound in his flank. He pulled a pillow close to his incision and seemed to doze. Then he said, "It will be like being blinded, not to be able to see the various possible futures. But go ahead, Tavistock, put it on."

"We'd like to check it out first." Tavistock suspected the device was a ruse.

Quince said, "I'd like one. I know what some people say about the fan of future possibilities, how we can pick one of the nicer possible futures and do things to make it happen even if it's not the most likely of futures, but I can't steer my way to make a small good potential future into the way that really happens. The obvious bad big potential futures are what will happen."

Vel didn't open his eyes when he said, "That's not true." An old argument between them, Tavistock thought. They'd said these things before without convincing each other, so now it was just verbal call and response.

Quince said, "Now, you're not going to die."

Tavistock said, "Don't you want to get whoever shot your father?" He decided to put the device on Vel's ankle.

If it was a ruse, perhaps he should play along for now. He pulled the sheet back, put it on Vel's ankle, and keyed it closed, using his anniversary as the code. They'd have to generate a better code later, but the biometrics would be an added protection against tampering, if the device really used biometrics. So now either Vel couldn't time-jump, or he could pretend that he couldn't. Or something.

Vel said, "I got him. In another time and country." He still hadn't opened his eyes. "You know, this is a bit restful."

"Who really invented it?"

"I don't know. Diana apparently can block Quince, throw shit in Quince's mind."

Quince said, "She showed me Dad with his brains out. When you're done with it, I'd like to try it. I hate seeing all the futures' variants waiting for me."

Tavistock felt particularly short-lived then, and confused. "Why did you kill whoever?"

"He was trying to kill me."

"God thing. You wouldn't understand," Quince said.

Vel said, "Can we talk about this later? I hurt, and they're going to make me walk again before dinner."

Tavistock felt like the youngest person in the room, tired and bewildered. He wondered how his team could keep Vel safe from people who could teleport into his room, from poorly socialized teenage seers. Maybe the device was some piece of bullshit that would let Vel skip a few centuries until he found a time that thought the records Tavistock's team was leaving were so much fantasy. Perhaps the whole thing was some elaborate hoax? What did this mean for security? Whatever. Tavistock still hadn't shared the video. He also wanted to spare

Quince seeing her father being raped, but perhaps she wasn't that delicate.

Back at his flat, Tavistock logged his hours on the new billing code and wondered about Vel's insistence that the future wasn't fixed. Futures. He took off his jeans and shirt, showered, and fell asleep until Isobel came home with Patrick, then dressed and ate dinner with them, played video games while Isobel and Patrick played with a ball on the floor, her long hair swinging with her body and arms pushing the ball back to Patrick. Isobel and Patrick quit playing with the ball and grabbed Tavistock's hands. Isobel took the computer away from him while Patrick tickled him, then they rolled in a family ball on the floor until Patrick was breathless and ready for bed. After they got Patrick to sleep, Tavistock strapped on his wrist baby monitor so he and Isobel could go into the walled garden behind the flats and play hide and seek with bamboo flutes sending soft cues from behind hedges and tree trunks until ten o'clock.

In the morning, Tavistock went to the office and met with the team. Cooper was sitting in again. Tavistock said, "He survived the night; he survived what he said was contact with a cousin. I couldn't stop that. His daughter was terrified of the other woman. He's relatively cooperative. I don't know where the device came from or if it really works, but if it gives off any electromagnetic signature, we might see if there are other devices like it anywhere. And did I say the daughter is a contact telepath. She did some thought insertion on the security people at the hospital."

Dora said, "I'll give you something to check any electromagnetic signatures."

Simon said, "We've been watching the video of the woman who came into his room. We can't figure out how... you saw it live?"

"Yes."

"So there are others?" Dora said.

"Obviously...apparently so. He said he was shot in a quarrel with another one like him, though not in our jurisdiction. Self-defense, and the other one is dead. The woman who was standing over him gave me the device that she said would contain him. I don't know if this is bullshit or not, but I put it on him. Looks like a monitoring anklet." Tavistock leaned back in his chair and looked at the drop ceiling tiles over the conference room table. The roof had leaked at some time, and the mold stains looked like giant goth kisses in black lipstick. Budget considerations, and they were up against people who had expensive friends and lawyers, and this one could jump in time and space.

"He has to be a natural phenomenon."

Tavistock laughed, thinking of girl telepaths with multicolored hair dyes. "Are we going to try him? How do we hold someone in prison if he can time-jump while shot? How much pain, what drugs to hold him?"

Cooper said, "I'd rather have him on our side, working for us. How reliably can he time-jump?"

"I don't know. The daughter says she'll be working for the Home Office next year."

"She can only work two hours a week at that age," Cooper said. "We'd rather have him. And we're going to have another team interrogating her."

Dora said, "I've never believed that telepathy through space was possible, but contact, direct experience of another person's sensorium—"

Tavistock said, "I'd like to be able to block it. Only way now is to make sure she doesn't touch me. Maybe resistant clothes? I don't know if she has to touch skin or not." He took a deep breath and said, "He sent me a video before he was shot."

"We know. Shouldn't we have heard about it earlier?" Marcus said. He fiddled with his cell phone, not looking at Tavistock.

"I don't know what it means, if it's real, when it happened if it is real. He's raped."

Simon said, "His family's luck isn't good for him, and not that good for them. He hasn't made them powerful or rich."

Cooper said, "Actually, he's made them quite comfortable. I didn't know antique dealers made that much. The rest of the family we've been able to trace has done well, just not ostentatiously rich. But I can't imagine that he survived for thousands of years on charm and compound interest alone."

Dora said, "We got the video off your drive, Joe. Don't hide things from us in the future."

No secrets in a secret organization, Tavistock thought. He said, "His doctor, mother of his child, says she suspects he wants something from us. What, she doesn't know."

Cooper said, "If he wants something from us, we should get something from him."

Tavistock said, "Isn't Quince something?"

"Depends on what he wants," Cooper said. "And what we find out about her."

The group drifted off-topic into a discussion of grey-hound racing and speculated on whether Vel's versions of the futures were crisp enough to influence dog bets. At lunchtime, Tavistock and Marcus went by Vel's London shop, which was open despite what had happened to him. The shop's clerks bore a family resemblance, dark curly hair, and faintly olive complexions. Tavistock and Marcus went on to a handy Pakistani place that wasn't just take-away.

"If you feel too close to him," Marcus said, holding a rolled-up roti near his mouth, "Cooper said we could take you off the case."

"I was the one who found the case."

"Well, there is that. And we are trying to get him to cooperate with us, and he opened up to you. We don't know what he represents. Or what the complications would be of pissing him off."

Tavistock went home to his own fussy child who at four seemed delightfully normal compared to Quince, though unlike Quince, he'd age and die within the next hundred years without some medical breakthrough. His mother was busy with a knitting project, sitting on the couch with the television on, but not paying any attention to it or to her son and husband.

Tavistock scooped Patrick up and asked, "You want to ride on my feet?"

"Yeah," Patrick said. Tavistock lay down in front of the couch and lifted Patrick, his son's belly against the soles of his feet and, tossed Patrick onto the couch beside Isobel, interrupting her knitting. She looked down at him and smiled. Tavistock got Patrick balanced on his feet again and did baby leg lifts. He realized he hadn't done anything physical since Vel was shot. Patrick beamed down at him, happy with the attention.

"Busy at work?" Isobel asked.

"It's all mental," Tavistock said. "I'd rather have…"

The needles paused again, and she said, "Do let me know when you're going to be out late."

"Unexpected. I can bring you a note from the hospital."

"Hospital? If the telly is a bore, I've got a DVD of a Russian flick."

"I'll just play with Patrick until his bedtime. Is that okay with you, Patrick?" The boy squealed over his head, and Tavistock brought him down as low as possible and tried to curl up for a kiss. Not quite low enough.

"He's really being better. Doctor says it's not ADD at all, just being four. I was worried."

"I should spend more time with him. Maybe take him to Somerset." Tavistock thought having his son with him might break the ice at bit. But then, Vel had gotten shot. Who knew about feuds between the gods, even gods who weren't like the recent past's concept of a God with a capital G who was far more abstract than the man lying in the hospital bed?

"You're a good father."

"I don't know if it would be useful to me to be able to talk to you about work. But you asked me not to bring work home." Tavistock thought, *If she had a clearance…*, but she cut the thought in half with what she said next.

"Work simply makes pleasures and ceremonies possible. And work won't remember you after you're gone. People who've shared pleasures and ceremonies remember."

She couldn't get a clearance. Too many oddities in her past, school leaving, the hippie parents, lack of birth records. Tavistock loved her better for forcing him to keep a life separate from work. The secrets stayed in the office. "When Patrick's older, I'll teach him video games. We can both teach him music."

"I love you. Remember that. You've been an easy man to live with. I'm glad I let you take me away from the trout-fishing bore. He told me I didn't know my own mind."

"A woman who casts with a Tonkin cane rod knows her own mind," Tavistock replied. He tossed Patrick gently onto the sofa beside her. She got up from the sofa and kissed him on his eyelids. He kissed her back, two kisses for each eyelid, her lashes flicking against his lips.

Tavistock asked Carolyn, Vel's doctor, if he could talk to her. Yes, she could meet him in the afternoon after she'd had a bit more sleep.

They'd meet away from the hospital, at her office. Tavistock wondered if it would be one of those modern efficient doctor's offices with no visible decorations other than drug manufacturer calendars and plastic chairs, or if it would be one of the old style surgeries with heaps of magazines and worn chintz covered sofas and armchairs.

It was neither, but furnished with tropical hardwood chairs with woven seats and backs, a desk for the receptionist, and racks of newspapers and magazines. On the wall were printouts of photographs of Vel's house and the Crescent at Bath. The floor was tile, and the waiting room smelled slightly of bleach.

Carolyn came out and looked at Tavistock, then nodded at him and said, "If you'd come this way." Tavistock followed her into a small office with a window on a planted courtyard. The furniture was very much like the furniture in the waiting room, all tropical hardwoods, but in somewhat more contemporary styles. "Vel wants us to cooperate. I've been on the phone with Emil's practice trying to get him a few more days off in six weeks when Vel can appreciate his company more. That is, if you're going to let us take Vel home for convalescence."

"We haven't decided yet."

"He's afraid that you're going to dissect him."

"That explains why he didn't want general anesthesia for the debriding procedure."

"Humor him on that one. I'm sure your people have considered letting him die in surgery and just disappear. The stress of worrying wouldn't be good for him. People have died of thinking they would die."

"The family has been using him for thousands of years to dodge plagues, natural disasters, and the worst alliances politically. Your luck, the poor bastard."

"I wondered why you seemed more hostile to us than to him. DNA scans came back with a common maternal ancestor?"

Tavistock realized that as a doctor she'd know what samples they could get easily. "We had samples of Quince from her birth umbilical blood samples. Since Quince shares a common maternal ancestor with him, so do you."

"Terribly embarrassing for him if he had been taking care of strangers for all those thousands of years," Carolyn said. She laughed very briefly.

"What do you want for him?"

"I want him to have a life outside a cage or under drugs. I want him to be able to go back to his mammoth farm and Emil and set up how he's going to evade the glacier that he sees coming to England in the next thousand years or so. What did he do that pissed his cousins off enough that one tried to kill him?"

"One was at the hospital. She wanted to know if he was making a habit out of killing gods. Said she'd have ripped his brains out if he had."

"I've never met another one. He's told us tales about one or two of them. I don't think they're genetically able to breed with each other, or they'd have taken over the planet."

"We have someone on staff that could test that."

"I would be too squicked to combine Vel's and Quince's gametes."

"No, I understand. We'd like him to work for us. He'd make a great asset."

"You're getting Quince. Why, I don't know. She can pick futures wisely enough to avoid trouble in cabs or buses or walking, but she's being absolutely theatrical about how her relationships will suck and she can't change anything at all."

"She's thirteen."

"She's thirteen going on 20,000. I believe I'm the only person she can't read, which is probably my only gift. I thought I didn't have any."

"Was the family trying to breed another Vel?"

"Yes. But Quince isn't another Vel."

Tavistock waited a moment. Carolyn stared over his head at a wall, as she spoke. "Vel recovers a bit slower than other humans, just more thoroughly. I often thought his mother must have done an excellent job of cultivating his basic stability. I haven't been as good with Quince. Vel's so easy going most of the time and basically good-natured that I forgot that the classic and Norse gods weren't all nice. Live a long time, bully the dying ones."

Tavistock said, "I think I'd have gone mad, losing everyone, knowing that everyone I loved would die before I did."

"He has his family. We're individually like pearls on a thread, I think, but he has us."

"He said his family kept him sane."

"He's Uncle Vel who makes the Yule fire, and he's the father of my child. I didn't think that would matter so much. Sperm donor, not my partner."

"The hospital said that the only thing that could kill him now would be a massive infection."

"And his liver reacts to antibiotics. I asked them to do daily liver enzyme checks. Once he's produced enough of his own blood, antibiotics are unnecessary, though I do understand that right after surgery, he was full of bog-standard O positive and the antibiotics probably were necessary."

"The arrowhead the surgeon pulled out—the tissue around it, nearest to the arrowhead, was something like 12,000 years old."

"He guesses he was born 14,000 years ago. You can't deport him to his birthplace. Where he was born is now under the North Sea."

Tavistock said, "We have photos from 1951, but he looked young then."

"He goes through adolescence periodically. Sheds body hair and teeth, grows new ones. And is really a handful then, for a year or two. Some cerebral reorganization, too, I suspect. He condenses or forgets centuries. I've seen him through one rejuvenation. Not fun for either of us.

He says the horror is being an adult trapped in the brain and body of a fourteen-year-old."

"Has he always been hidden?"

"No. Once upon a time, he was something like a local brownie. Even in Christian times, early Christian times at least in Somerset, the priests explained that he had no soul but didn't try to kill him. Christians told him that when he died, what he'd been would vanish into air. Other people had a different kind of immortality than he did, had hell or heaven. He seems to have let all the theories—god, sprite, whatever—go unchallenged. I don't know if he believed any of them. What he does is tell his family stories. After decades of listening to Uncle Vel, I realized that the stories were more about the present, reinventing himself. He has had huge gaps in his stories, maybe times when what happened was too boring to remember."

"Or too awful," Tavistock said, thinking about the video. "Thanks for cooperating with us. I'll try to make sure he can stay awake for the debriding."

"My daughter needs her father, Mr. Tavistock. You people will get a sane asset if you let him help her learn how to live."

"Feel free to call me Joe. Here's my card."

Carolyn showed him out beyond the room where she now had patients waiting, ready to return to her professional role.

Tavistock took a cab to the hospital where he was scheduled to meet with the medical team to discuss Vel's progress. Dora had sent over the device that would capture any electromagnetic signatures the device might emit. He thought he'd check in on Vel before the meeting, but was running a bit late. The team had a cleared sitter; the family had its representative. He took the elevator up to the surgeon's usual ward and then asked where his office was.

Yet another "the world all looks alike" office, Tavistock thought as he sat down on a metal folding chair pulled up to a metal table that was being the conference table right now and which probably was also used to sort medical supplies and to set up lunches. The nurses were waiting for the surgeon, who wasn't as cleared as they were. One of them said, "I think he's guessing, but he doesn't want to know."

The surgeon came in late, still wearing a surgical gown with blood on it. He said, "Sorry, sorting out a car crash. About Vel, I'd like it if he was a bit further along, but it's pretty typical to debride the entrance and exit wounds four days after repair. Then we let those wounds heal by granulation, pack them gently, and let them heal from the inside out."

One of the nurses said, "He's sloughing off dead tissue. Cultivating fluids coming off don't show any bacteria. Swabbing has been getting out a fair amount of dead matter. Healing generally seems a bit slower than usual, though."

Tavistock said, "Is there any medical reason for doing it under general anesthesia rather than a local?"

The surgeon said, "It's more comfortable for the patient. We do tugging and scraping. Some patients make pests of themselves if they're awake."

"Can you humor him on this? He doesn't want general anesthesia."

"Sedate him a bit and do a spinal block. He won't be moving," the nurse said.

"Yes, we could do that. And he might recover faster without the general."

Tavistock went upstairs to the locked rooms to tell Vel he wouldn't be under general anesthesia for the debriding procedure and to run Dora's device over his anklet. He found Vel and Emil kissing, Vel flat on the bed, holding the back of Emil's head. "Am I interrupting anything?"

Vel moved Emil's head back and said, "Yes."

One of the nurses came in behind Tavistock and said to Vel, "You really can't do anything with that hard-on for six weeks, you know. Emil, your hospital says you can take a few more days off in six weeks if you do some overtime between now and then. Here, the family is paying for this and sent it over." She handed Emil an envelope.

Emil opened the envelope and pulled out an airline ticket. "I could have paid for this."

"Yes, but the family wanted to. Joe, let's leave them to finish saying good bye."

Moments later, in the hall, Tavistock told Emil that they'd use a spinal block for the debriding and the bullet wounds. Emil said, "Thanks. If you do decide to kill him for any reason, please give him the grace of letting him die conscious."

"You're being melodramatic."

Emil stared at him. Tavistock thought, now that's an incredulous look.

After Emil had gone, Tavistock waited in the recovery room to see Vel after the debriding procedure. He'd bill for some of this time, but not all of it, not the waiting. A man in a suit who appeared to be yet another one of Vel's family members was waiting.

Vel came back a bit loopy from the sedative. "I worried too much, didn't I?" he said to Tavistock.

Tavistock said, "We followed what you wanted. Would you have rather been asleep?"

The surgeon said, "Not much dead tissue left. As the nurse said, his body had been sloughing it off. Nice clean tissue bed for healing."

"My cock is numb. I can move, but my whole lower belly is numb. How long does this last?"

The surgeon said, "Eight hours, but you can move."

Vel said, "It didn't hurt."

"That's the purpose of the spinal block," the surgeon said. "The sedative was to keep you from worrying about the tugging sensations."

"I tried to not say anything while you were working."

The surgeon looked at Tavistock and then back at Vel. "You were very good. I'll see you upstairs in the morning after my downstairs rounds. Mr. Tavistock."

Tavistock followed the surgeon out of the recovery room. The surgeon said, "He's in custody, isn't he? Where are you going to transfer him? He should have a visiting nurse to help with dressings and to monitor his condition. If he were a typical city patient, we'd be releasing him to family if they were willing to take him in or to a convalescence home if he didn't have family."

Tavistock said, "He is in custody. We haven't decided quite where to send him. Can he stay here until he's fully mobile?"

"A convalescence home with grounds where he could be outside and get some exercise would be better. You could send people to watch him."

Vel's family representative said, "We'd like to take him back to the house in Somerset."

Tavistock said, "Our people are talking with your solicitor about bond."

"Can I bring in his laptop once he's a bit better?"

"Call me and we'll screen it before he can have it." Once on the pavement, he called Carolyn to let her know the debriding process went well. She said, "I can understand his pain. He's like any other human when he's hurting. I can understand his lusts. He goes outside himself, just like us. Transcends the difference. Otherwise, I don't know whether he really is like us or if he's an excellent chameleon."

"Wouldn't think that he'd have picked being gay if he was trying to be a perfect imitation of a man of whatever times."

"I suspect that for most of human history, that more kept him out of trouble with other people's fathers and husbands than got him into trouble. I asked him what the average attitude for being gay was over all those years. He said that most cultures thought it was a bit silly. He could live with being a bit silly."

"I can't promise anything." Tavistock closed his phone and went back upstairs to scan Vel's device, then sent Dora's machine back to her.

Dora called to say that the woman in the video at Vel's hospital room had shown up in her office, saying that she needed to take part in a test of embryo viability. Tavistock called Carolyn to say that they would be able to run the viability test on Vel and someone who had his traits who wasn't Quince.

Carolyn said, "I've got frozen semen. I'll be over as soon as you have a procedure room ready. The hospital where Vel is?"

"No, you'll be coming to one of our facilities. We'll send a car."

Carolyn said, "You know the advantage of finding out that they can't breed with each other is huge."

"Yeah, like Manx cats and harlequin Great Danes. Tell me what the advantage is again?"

"They can't get rid of us. If they don't know that, they need to know that."

Tavistock had to sit down for a moment. He called Marcus and told him that they needed to pick up a semen sample and doctor.

When he got to the facility, Dora opened the door for them and said, "I believe you met earlier."

The woman held out her hand to Tavistock and said, "I'm Diana Younger." Tavistock didn't touch her. She had to have been a contact telepath to know that Vel didn't make a habit of killing his own kind and to put thoughts in Quince's mind.

"Can I see your passport?" Cooper would have to clear asking the Americans if they knew who this woman was.

"I don't carry my passport when I'm jumping. That would be stupid. I'm not Vel. And I'm leaving as soon as you take an egg or two. I'm currently ovulating."

"Do you know what the results will be?"

"Yes, that's why I didn't kill Vel on general principles."

"Humor us," Carolyn said. "Let's do the test anyway. Gods can lie."

Tavistock asked, "Is there any way to spread the word about this to other people like you and Vel?"

"I'm not the secretary for the gods, you know."

Tavistock didn't know if she was bullshitting him or being honest. Carolyn, with her gift protecting her from contact telepaths, helped Diana on to the obstetrics table.

"You're unreadable? Bitch."

"Being unreadable helped lots with raising Quince." Carolyn harvested two eggs, took a snip of general tissue, and then put a bandage over the puncture hole.

The zygotes burnt out in a nodule of almost cancerous tissue under the microscope that fed into the monitor they all were watching. Dora set up a DNA sequence to compare with Vel's and said, "We could get back to you with printed results on how the DNA was abnormal if you gave us an address."

"I don't need further results, and you don't need my address. My father was like you, Carolyn, a man with some talent but not long-lived. Carrier."

Tavistock said, "So, magic is genetic."

Diana said, "It's something in how cellular repair is done."

"Apparently, as we've noticed with Vel," Dora said as she wrote labels for the test material. "But I'm not sure of the bio-mechanics of the time-jumping."

"Me, neither," Diana said as she picked a spot where time changed for her but not for them. She left words dangling in the air as she stepped through. "Not my specialty."

Tavistock had an image of the gods on a listserv, warning each other about what the dying ones were up to now. Dora said, "I think she took fertility drugs so we could be sure to harvest eggs, but the zygote development was seriously abnormal, even taking that into consideration. We're running the videos we've got against facial photograph databases."

Cooper said, "We were considering vivisection, yes. We'd have taken you and the surgeon off the case once he was under anesthesia, but we realized after talking to Quince that we couldn't pass it off as an accidental death. So, we didn't. He could have been under general anesthesia for the procedure without any fear. Carolyn said he wanted something from us. We need to ask him what he wants from us."

"You know not to touch Quince, don't you?"

"We interviewed her in the presence of her mother and attorney, and yes, we read your report. We'd rather have the father, but there are, after all, huge gaps in his history. And I suspect he's rather shell-shocked after all that's happened to him. If he were sent off to do something dangerous, no telling where he'd jump. She can't time-jump, so we can keep track of her. He's a more powerful potential asset; she's both willing and more controllable. A month ago, I would have thought all this was insane."

Tavistock said, "You can raise this godlet from a child, or at least teenager."

Cooper smiled. "Her hair is orange now. Her mother says she needs her father's guidance. She's impressive enough. Read a Farsi-speaking volunteer, and we don't think she knew the language. The prediction of the futures is a bit less impressive, could be just visualization of her own speculations rather than anything more real. Gets vague on the national level. We can't use her on actual prisoners until we find a way to make them amnesiac for the event."

Tavistock said, "The hospital wants to know what our plans are for him."

Cooper said, "I did read your report. We aren't going to put him in a general prison hospital, but we need to finish interrogating one of his family members we found in MI5, a woman. She's offered to resign, claims she speculated about Vel, but thought she might be committed if she tried to talk about it. Claims she's not spying for him. We'd like you to take her photograph and show it to Vel, see what his reaction is. Only two of his family shows up in the convict DNA database, minor thefts as teenagers, but having one of his family in MI5's employee DNA database complicates this." Cooper slid a photo mailer over to Tavistock. "I appreciate that you've been visiting him without billing for it, but this will be billable time. Don't get too close to him. You're not that good an interrogator, though he does seem to trust you for some reason."

Tavistock said, "I thought I was a systems analyst."

"You're a better interrogator than Marcus, and we've got technical people enough," Cooper said.

Vel was sitting up in a chair reading a P.D. James novel when Tavistock came by with the photograph. He didn't say anything to Vel, just opened the mailer and pulled out the photograph. Vel said, "An official visit?"

"With billable hours. Recognize her?"

"She comes to the Yule parties with her husband and child. They married at the house one Yule. Does she know about me? She's not one of the people I told. She's got some kind of government job that she really loves but doesn't talk about much, so I thought it would be prudent not to tell her my secrets if she couldn't tell me hers."

"You didn't plant her in MI5?"

"No. Wouldn't need to. Quince can see what the probabilities are for the damn planet. I can see what the probabilities are for me except for this period when I'm wearing this stupid-ass device."

"You're not being charming right now."

"I'm not feeling well. I'm still sore from the gunshot and the surgery, and—"

"—you could see into this time before we put the device on you."

"No, I couldn't. Quince could. I suspect the Diana could. And if you try to put one of these things on Quince, we will have all the lawyers trying to stop you unless Quince says okay. Lots of luck in catching Diana."

"We're going to continue interrogating the woman. She's offered to resign."

"I can't warn my people not to take government jobs because the family has secrets—I don't make their choices for them. Was she a good officer? Did she see through some of the American forgeries about Iraqi weapons of mass destruction?"

"I don't know."

"I hope she did a good job and didn't do anything stupid. I'm sorry if she loses the job because of me. You can believe me or not, but I didn't plant her with you. I need to get some sunshine. Please let me go home." He stopped talking and sat staring at his feet for a while. "I'm whining. Sorry. My liver started quarreling with the antibiotics. I didn't realize all this would hurt so much for so long. Crap day."

Tavistock believed him about his kinswoman. They needed him to help with Quince, who came up with paired solicitors with appropriate clearances now every time anyone from an agency talked to her. He'd try to get permission to take Vel outside, perhaps to lunch.

Vel said, "It's not physically painful, the device, but it's like being blinded. I've been physically blinded before, but my eyes grew back. I think if they'd burned the sockets, they wouldn't have."

"Vel, don't play me."

"Please let me go home. And please don't hurt my kinswoman."

"You really didn't know she was in MI5?"

"I guessed she was with one of the spooky agencies. What was I supposed to do?"

Tavistock sat with Vel, not saying anything, waiting for Vel to say more. Vel closed his eyes and said, "Not knowing what could be coming is actually a bit restful, considering, but only a bit."

"I've got to go back to the office and enter these billable hours, make my report, and go home to my own family."

Still with his eyes closed, sitting in the chair, Vel asked, "Children?"

"A four-year-old boy. Favors his mother in some ways."

Vel opened his eyes. He almost said something, but closed his eyes again. "You understand families then."

"They're my refuge from work. My wife brings me ceremonies and pleasure."

"Mine are my work, and my refuge."

"You were their luck. You could always whore for pizza in Atlanta if the game was scarce."

Vel opened his eyes at that. They looked darker than usual. "I made sure they never starved if they listened to me. And I did what I had to do to get them to listen."

"Vel, one thing I can assure you of is that we're not going to take you apart to see what makes you tick."

"It wouldn't be British to kill a man for forging his passport in peace time."

Tavistock found himself liking Vel, but he knew Vel survived by making himself likeable, by getting people to trust him. *Charm and compound interest.* Time to go home.

At home, Isobel, in a long dress cut to be clinging, was sitting with Patrick in her arms. Tavistock couldn't tell her anything, but she seemed to recognize his grimness. She kissed the tip of his nose, then bowed her head for a full mouth kiss. She'd never gotten a passport, said that London was travel enough for her.

If Vel hadn't wanted to travel by mortal transportation, Tavistock would never have discovered the passport anomalies.

"Difficult at work."

"Yeah, I can say that much."

"Come cuddle with us, and I'll sing you both a story."

Tavistock cuddled her while she cuddled their son and sang them a story about a good fairy in Wales who churned butter while milk maids dallied with their lovers, who fixed shoes left on the doorsteps at night, who hid during the day and never let anyone see whoever's face. The good fairy tickled trout from the streams and called the geese down from the skies.

Tavistock's heart curled up in his chest. He realized she might have been born far earlier than the hippies who'd claimed her as their child with no papers.

He should recuse himself from Vel's case. But if he did, like the woman in MI5, he'd have no end of problems, and who would believe him on anything having to do with Vel, mortal husband of an immortal? His team's first thought would be that Vel had sent Isobel to his bed. He wanted to ask her not to leave him when he got old, and how much Patrick took after her. Did she know Vel? Or was he imagining things, seeing fairies everywhere now that he knew Vel existed?

She kissed him on the nose again before she took Patrick off to his cot.

When Isobel came back, Tavistock remembered how scar-free her body had been and still was. He whispered in her ear, hoping the devices in the house couldn't pick up what he was saying, "Did your fairy churn butter or mend shoes?"

"Ah, my story," Isobel whispered back, and led him off to bed where her vagina milked him dry and utterly satisfied, like a man in love with the Fairy Queen. La Belle Dame, with mercy. He forgot himself in her. The ones who didn't make the mythology books were the wisest of the immortals. She held him in her arms until he was almost asleep, then whispered in his ear, "Never bring work home."

Vel had sent him the tape for a reason. Tavistock hoped that he hadn't sent Isobel. Or had Isobel sent herself, and if so, why?

Isobel ran the index finger of her left hand around his navel. "Have I told you how much I love living with you and Patrick," she said.

"Yes, and I love you both, too." Realizing what she was turned her from being a break from work to work's most terrible complication. If Vel had sent her to seduce him, Tavistock would hate Vel. He almost said, "Somerset was a part of Wales once," but he knew that would come out too hostile, too much a clue for the listeners. Perhaps Vel is corrupting me, Tavistock thought as he drifted off to sleep.

The team met again with Cooper to discuss Vel. Cooper said, "I've been talking to some very discreet higher -ups. We're not unjust or arbitrary, and we're going to try to be as sympathetic as possible to him. We aren't the police who destroyed Alan Turing. Times have changed. Vel had good reasons to hide earlier. He doesn't have a reason to hide now, but he needs to repay us for the passport fraud and working for us would work. We tried to get the Americans to identify Diana, but they aren't talking to us, so I imagine she's making her own arrangements with them. She'd also be a great asset if she wanted to be. We've got facial recognition software trolling Google Images and our own image databases."

Tavistock didn't say anything.

"Quiet today, Joe," Dora said.

"I don't think he planted his kinswoman in MI5, but I suspect I believe that because I rather like him."

Simon said, "He couldn't have survived all that time without being ruthless at least at times."

Tavistock said, "He couldn't have survived all that time if he made too many enemies."

Dora said, "Twelve thousand years ago, plus or minus 500 years, someone put this in him." She pushed a small pasteboard box with an elastic band attached to the lid toward Tavistock, who opened it.

He lifted the top layer of cotton wadding and saw that the arrowhead was quartz, a tiny thing with a tiny gold occlusion in the bulb. "Smaller than I'd imagine anyone would choose for man-killing." The tip looked fragile, rippled with the patience of whoever had beaten the two edges sharp and serrated, tiny chip after tiny chip.

Dora said, "Our flint knapping consultant says it's typical of very late Paleolithic. The knapper used a bone or horn baton to chip the edges, but didn't polish it. Being made of quartz, especially with the gold occlusion in the bulb on the non-pointed end, suggests a ritual object or an eccentric knapper. Obsidian is often found to have been used for these sorts of projectiles, especially in the New World. The earliest layers of calcium date back, haven't been biologically active the way bone is."

"Ritual object to kill a god? Or control him with pain?" Tavistock said. He laid the arrowhead back on the bottom layer of cotton, then covered it again and closed the box.

Simon said, "It's almost like jewelry. Odd to actually use it."

Tavistock wondered if the little arrowhead might have been the very late Paleolithic's equivalent of the device on Vel's ankle. "I'll ask him about it, if you let me take it with me."

Cooper nodded. Tavistock also wanted to ask Vel how he dealt with mortal lovers, what his or Quince's sight had shown him about Isobel, and what he represented to Vel, but even thinking about those things in Cooper's presence made him uneasy.

When he got to the hospital, Vel was reading on a laptop. He looked up at Tavistock. "Billable hours again?"

"Yeah. Can I interrupt?"

"Hope you don't mind the laptop. Your people cleared it, and it's not connected to the net."

"Someone tried to kill you or hurt you once, with an arrowhead that was in a calcium nodule the surgeon removed when he had you open. Not recent. A long time ago." Tavistock pulled out the box, opened the lid, and took off the top layer of cotton batting and passed the box to Vel.

"Someone could have decided I'd be good to eat. You must have dated it. Where? When?"

"Under your left pelvic crest. About 12,000 years ago, plus or minus 500 years."

Vel picked the projectile out of the box, cautiously, by the bulb, and carefully rubbed his finger over a cutting edge, not along it. "It's still razor sharp. Twelve thousand years ago, plus or minus, is one of my big memory gaps. I've been going back to set camera traps for times I have no or confusing memories of. The Younger Dryas was one of them. I'll have to have someone get the videos to your people."

"They know already that you sent a video to me earlier."

"Ah, we're in that future, then."

"Can you see my futures?"

"I'm not Quince." He kept the arrowhead in his hand, then moved his fingers off the bulb and saw the gold inclusion in the arrowhead. "Ritual object. To control me. I was hurt in the video."

"Has the anklet bothered you?"

"My futures looked so chaotic recently that not seeing hasn't really been that bad. But I do feel a bit like a mouse in a hawk trap. You couldn't keep the Diana out. I'm taking it on faith that the device would keep her from reaching inside me."

"You're being guarded here. We'll shoot her if she shows up again. If we decide to let you go home for recovery, we'll send guards there. We want to make a larger scale version of the device the Diana gave us, but this has got to be on your ankle for now. Of course, all this could be the gods toying with us."

"You take yourselves too seriously," Vel said. "We're not that complicated. Most of us were actually only average in intelligence, a few stupid. Quince thinks I'll be safe enough at the house."

Tavistock hesitated to ask his other question. "When you were in deep hiding, both because you wouldn't age and because your orientation was illegal, how long could you stay with a man? You seem to have longer-term lovers now."

"I had to move on before they noticed or compared notes." He paused, looking down at the now closed box. "You all die, but if I'm a comfort to a dying man I love, I'd be with him."

"Couldn't you be with one of your own?"

Vel sighed and handed the box back to me. "My own kind? I stay sane by being with the nieces and nephews, not the cousins. It's painful to bury, but—this is going to sound demeaning, but I love your kind like people love dogs. Dogs die, but dog lovers don't stop keeping dogs. You're much more than dogs to me, really. I remember the good times, and don't focus on the dying."

Tavistock thought but didn't say, But our lives were tiny fractions of what dogs' lives were to humans.

Vel said, "One other thing. Mostly I live in the present. My life is longer than yours, but my seconds are neither shorter nor longer. On an average day, I try not to think about the past or the future. Sell antiques, take care of the family children, the farm, and love my lovers."

"So you take mortal lovers, and they die."

"Didn't you hear what I said? I don't take them to watch them grow old and die. I live with them while they're alive. In some eras, I was with sons of one family for several centuries, more for the men's families than for the men, sometimes."

"Would you want to live like that again?"

"If I could, yes. I'd be the continuity for two families. But with modern comforts."

"Some of your cousins, as you call them, may do it differently."

"I can't speak for the cousins. I avoid them. The few that I've met see this obsession with my sister's family as silly." Vel turned off the laptop and sat so long in his own thoughts that Tavistock guessed Vel had to filter what he remembered into this current language, English. "I've outlived the major Olympians. I think I made the right decision. Carolyn said that when I'm finally dead, it won't have mattered how long I lived. I can't die of old age. I'll die of stupidity, treachery, or some dumb accident I can't see how to avoid. Or I'll decide to take the car crash or bullet so one of you short-lived people can have a little bit longer in the sun."

"So there's not an Old Gods Club?"

"I don't know. I'm certainly not part of such a thing."

"La Belle Dame Sans Merci?"

"No. I'm not the queer equivalent of that. I had very short-term relationships when I had to leave people to avoid being found out. I prefer life partners. Look, my brain isn't bigger than your brain. I can't remember everything that happened to me for all sorts of reasons. I've got an IQ of around 140, not thousands. I've found a reason to live that works for me. I suspect that the surviving cousins have worked out similar strategies. We'd be old fogies trapped in the past that formed us if we only talked to each other. The short-lived change so much so often."

"'The dying ones.'"

"That phrase tends to go with the wrong attitude."

"You've killed your own kind."

"Yes. Do you want details? I don't think either happened in your jurisdiction, Mr. Tavistock."

"Why?"

"To protect my family." Vel seemed to be getting very tired now.

"I don't think you'd want Quince to see that video."

"Thanks."

"Did you have any particular reason to send it to me?"

"You were going to find the passport anomalies, at least in most of my possible futures, so I thought if you saw it, you could believe me without a huge amount of fuss and self-doubt and wondering if either or both of us were insane. I'm going to need your help. That explains some of why. Quince knows more about what's coming than I do, but she's pissed with me at the moment. She'd be seriously angry if I died anytime soon."

"What about the minor goddesses, the nymphs and dryads?" Tavistock asked. Tavistock wanted and didn't want to ask if Vel had put a spy in his bed. "Yes" would be too horrible, and Tavistock wouldn't have trusted a denial.

Vel said, "Some of the women give their mortal lovers a child before they leave. So I've heard. I've never met any. They're just legends as far as I'm concerned."

"Would the cousins care what happened to you now?"

Vel said, "I doubt they're all of one opinion on me, if they're many of them left. I probably look like I've gotten us all into stupid trouble now. I'm tired, Joe, or are you being Mr. Tavistock on the clock?"

Tavistock didn't answer that, but said, "I hope we decide to let you go back to your family." He was wondering when Isobel would leave him, if she could hide from the CCTV cameras, how long she'd been alive. He knew, without having Vel's or Quince's sight, that she would leave him and hoped that she did love him or had loved him. She'd given him eight years, a son, and a refuge from work in a comfortable house.

When Tavistock got home, Isobel was trying out a new electric spinning wheel. "It's an odd thing," she said. "Sort of like a back formation from contemporary technology to the older ways of production."

"Are you going to keep it?" Tavistock asked.

"Do you want me to?"

"If it makes you happy." Tavistock went into his office to write the report that said the arrowhead was of the same time frame as the video. Or so Vel said.

The next morning, Tavistock's team watched the video again, and Cooper was with them. Tavistock explained the rejuvenations, which was why Vel in the video looked adolescent. Simon said, "Looks like the nieces sold his ass for some testosterone-fueled muscle."

Dora said, "He's hurt, not just from the rapes."

Tavistock said, "The ritual arrowhead."

Simon said, "Maybe he enjoys it? Kink."

Marcus answered before Tavistock could. "No."

Tavistock said, "Submissive, but not that submissive. He set the camera traps because he couldn't remember."

Simon said, "You think he's a sub, Marcus?"

Tavistock answered, "A bit. His two recent lovers have been dominant men."

Simon said, "Before his last partner left him, he nearly bled out in a brothel in Amsterdam, knife play. Working as a rent boy. Did it for serious money, which the family almost spent down helicoptering him home."

"I hadn't heard those details," Tavistock said.

"He's obviously trying to curry your sympathy, and you're way too het to hear about that," Simon said.

"Guys, stop," Marcus said.

Cooper said, "What strategic advantages would a time traveler give us? And will he work honestly for us? That's the issue. He works for us; we do things for him."

Tavistock said, "The UK is not that relevant to him now. It's going to be run over by a glacier in a thousand years."

Cooper said, "We'll move. We've moved before. We could move to Slovakia if we had an advance base there."

Tavistock took the box with the arrowhead in it out of his pocket and put in on the table.

Marcus said, "So he's killed others of his kind to protect his family."

"But the Diana didn't think he was making a habit of it," Tavistock replied.

Cooper said, "Ask him who he killed besides this recent thing in self-defense."

Simon added, "Or so he claims it was self-defense."

Dora said, "Not that we have a body."

"Not more on-the-clock time," Vel said when Tavistock came in with the lunch tray.

"We want to know who you killed beside the one in this recent fracas."

"Zeus. He was killing women of my family. The cousins thought my preoccupation with these particular short-lived ones was funny."

"Where?"

"Where did he kill our girls or where did I kill him?"

"Both."

"He could time-jump but he didn't realize that where he couldn't see might be his death. Death doesn't show up as an option, apparently. He killed them in Somerset. Two. I knew his reputation for killing short-lived people, drowning one woman in urine. I got him in Greece. Had help. Found out he'd been bragging that he'd break me. I worried that other cousins were making trouble. Couldn't have done anything about the first killing, should have stopped him before the second." He took bites of food in the pauses between phrases and sentences. Tavistock let him say what he needed to say. Vel pushed the tray aside and stared at his hands. Vel turned them palm up, then rolled them back up and clenched them. "Didn't like doing it, but it was a time-binding thing. I guess I haven't explained that some times have no alternatives. Free will collapses. I just live the script, what happened happens."

"Fate?"

"It feels like a choice at the beginning. I suspect Zeus saw chances of escaping. I talked to one of the other cousins before he died. That one also didn't see any sign of his dying, just not so many futures." Vel stood up and walked to the toilet for a piss.

When he got back, Tavistock said, "You also say you killed the guy who shot you?"

"Yes. I have no real idea why he tried to kill me. Still, not in your jurisdiction or time."

"We haven't been able to produce a body."

"I barely made it back to present London. If the pain is too bad, if I'm drugged or really stoned or drunk, I can't move and I can barely see, just not as black as your device makes foresight. Why do your people want to make sure they can contain me?"

"Because you scare us." Tavistock knew that if he didn't speak for the others, he spoke for himself, something he hadn't been willing to admit before.

"Me? Scary?"

"You say you killed Zeus, remember? If Diana could really pluck brains out, you could, too."

"I'd even die to protect my family, but you're not threatening them, at least not that much. Quince wants to work for the Crown. I want to go back to my mammoth farm. But how long will she be a strategic secret? Having your armies clone contact telepaths and time-jumpers would be an interesting arms race. I know you've taken tissue samples. But people with major talents don't always play by the rules. We aren't always sane. Work with people who want to work with you and who are relatively sane."

"We're more interested in making the effects biologically transferable."

"If you could do it for all humans, I'd be in favor. Just some humans, and it's the same old arrogance on one side and nailing gods to trees on the other. Moving the gods into the abstract and reducing them to one and then making him vanish was genius."

Tavistock needed Vel to pull out of his introspection because what Vel said was making Tavistock uneasy, reminding him that Isobel had hinted at being another one of the cousins. "Well, I believe in you."

"Oh, please. Only time I got worshiped, some guy cut off the end of my left little finger when I was stoned—don't ask—and cauterized it. It didn't grow back until really recently, after Carolyn cut away the scar tissue and grafted in a new nail bed."

"Why not get it fixed earlier?

"I wanted to be reminded not to make that mistake again. It's seductive, being worshiped, staying stoned half the time. If I hadn't had the hash—"

"—would you still be a minor god somewhere being worshiped?"

"I needed to be driven away from that spring back to my family. A little bandit king cut off my fingertip and humiliated me in front of all the people who'd been sending me pigeons and sons earlier. After I was maimed, those people didn't help me or comfort me. They'd been too afraid to take me out themselves, but they'd been waiting for someone to fuck me up. Nobody.... I walked home alone. People remembered me back in Somerset, what was to become Somerset."

"Their luck was back."

"I'm Uncle Vel to my family, not a god, just a doubly queer sort of uncle."

"Are you tired?"

"Getting there. But I'd really like to go outside."

"Haven't they taken you to the roof exercise yard?"

"Yes. Thanks. But I'd like to walk among trees, on grass, not between walls topped with coils of razor wire."

"Would you like to go out to eat?"

Vel looked wistful. Tavistock wondered if he'd ever talked so frankly about what he was, what he'd been, and what he'd done to preserve being the family's luck. He was the man to whom Vel tried to explain himself; he wondered if Vel ever explained as much to family or the lovers who knew what he was. Probably not. "Take a nap. I can't promise anything, but I'll make a phone call."

The meal was neither lunch nor supper, just a break from the locked room and the roof-top exercise yard. Simon said, "It's not a date, is it?"

"No. I just thought he deserved a bit of a break from the room. I'm taking an orderly with us. And a wheelchair, if he gets too fatigued to walk."

"We'll call you back."

The decision took fifteen minutes. Vel and Tavistock sat in his room, not talking. Cooper gave them permission to go out with one of the cleared orderlies. The wheelchair went into the back of a cab, and Tavistock asked, "What would you like?"

"Sushi." Vel sat back cautiously on the cab seat, sandwiched between Tavistock and the orderly. Tavistock hadn't expected sushi, but after thinking about it a minute, the choice wasn't that surprising—raw flesh cut up, with rice, a combination of Paleolithic and Neolithic. The driver knew a place. Vel said he knew a better one, and Tavistock decided to take the chance.

The chef knew Vel, asked about the antique business. Vel said it was going well enough. The food was exquisite.

"I love miso soup," Vel said. "Even when the dashi isn't made from freshly shaved dried bonito fillets."

Tavistock could manage miso soup, but wasn't thrilled by the bits of seaweed. They left the wheelchair in the restaurant and walked around a bit under plane trees, naked trunks all white, peeling bark on the branches. Vel didn't need the wheelchair when they went back to the restaurant, but once they got back to the hospital, he let the orderly put him in it for the trip back to the locked room.

The surgeon had only cleaned the entry and exit wounds a week ago. The exit wound drained a bit after the trip out.

The next day, Peter Cooper brought the team together again to discuss Vel. He said, "The other agencies know relatively little. There's another work group I'm part of that reports to high-level security people in both agencies. No one wants this to get out to the American or German press. I'm not sure I can trust the other agencies, either. Diana's a Columbia University physical anthropology professor, very highly regarded, which Google Images gave up before someone scrubbed the images, but of course, we had our own archives of Google Images. The Americans sent a new guy to their UK Embassy, who has friends in government who are not in on any of this."

Tavistock wondered if those agencies kept their own secrets from his team for the same reasons.

Simon said, "If we transfer him to a prison hospital, we really lose control of the situation. His family has lawyers looking into the custody. They're asking us to do disclosure."

Tavistock said, "Send him home to the Somerset house. Make one of the conditions the family's discretion. Put everything under the Official Secrets Act, not that the Act would stop a person willing to be a martyr. Make them responsible for him. I also want to observe him interacting with them."

Cooper said, "In the wild, so to speak."

"They'll give us permission to bug the house. I also want to see more of his museum. It's apparently the way he holds what he can of his memories."

Simon said, "14,000 years."

Tavistock said, "He doesn't remember more than bits and pieces, apparently."

Cooper said, "How do we cover our arses if we've been conned about the containment device?"

Simon said, "We've been getting polite requests for information about his condition from all sorts."

Cooper said, "I'm fielding those, so pass them on to me. They shouldn't have any of our numbers. Tavistock, we had a team at the place the cabbie recommended, so why did you take him to another Japanese restaurant?"

"Being stupidly kind, I suppose," Tavistock said. "What do the doctors say?"

Dora said, "No sex for six weeks; no anal for six months; no lifting anything heavier than six pounds for three months; no running for three weeks without supervision. He'd probably do better at home, only his usual bedroom is upstairs in a tower. They could give him the bedroom behind the kitchen and move the current couple there up to one of the tower bedrooms. He'll probably be okay for climbing stairs four weeks after the incident, but the doctors are leaving a decision about that to his visiting nurse."

Marcus said, "We've ignored heroin use by rock stars. Maybe we can ignore this? He's a well-respected antique dealer who finds people things they've always wanted to find."

Simon said, "By going back in time and having the things made special."

Cooper said, "I'll sign off on getting the family to put the house and grounds up as collateral for his bond. Family might be touchy about that, but they've been asking for his release on bail. Not like we can expel him to his home country. He's been connected to Somerset since before this nation existed."

Tavistock came into Vel's room and said, "You're going to be released to your family until we make a final determination about what to do with you."

"I'm still not free to go where I want to go."

"Your solicitors and the Crown are still negotiating on where you can go. Do you have anything here? I'm going to drive you back to your house, and I'll be one of your monitors, probably Sunday through Tuesday. We've got

listening devices in your house now. I won't be there physically that often, but I'll be one of the people listening."

"I've got three suits with suspenders, loose in the
waist. I'll change to one of them. And two nightshirts.
Carolyn brought them in a duffel, but your people didn't
let me keep that."

After a nurse changed Vel's dressing, he put on one of
the suits. The orderly carried Vel's other clothes out over
his arm as they went for the elevator. They didn't say anything to each other as they rode the lift down to the base-
ment garage. The orderly folded the clothes in the trunk,
wrapping the suits in the nightshirts. Vel asked Tavistock
for directions for where to sit.

"We'll be in the back. The driver has a GPS with your
home location in it. We're restricting access to the arrest record on grounds of National Security. Your family put the
Somerset house and lands up as collateral for your bond."

"Yes. I heard. I'm cooperating. Please don't treat me
like a prisoner in front of my family."

Tavistock said, "I think I've been more than courteous. I almost got chewed out in front of other team members for taking you to your choice of Japanese restaurant."

Vel looked away from Tavistock and said, "You've
been courteous."

The car stopped for a break twenty miles beyond
Staines. The driver said that they could have lunch and
walk a bit.

After lunch, Vel, looking good in his suit, walked away
from Tavistock and the other two men, hands in his pockets, focused on the landscape. His eyes followed a hawk
to the horizon before he looked back at Tavistock's group
and stopped walking. The driver looked at Tavistock as if

ready to fetch Vel back to the car. Tavistock shook his head slightly. Vel turned back and joined the other men. "Goshawk," he said. "They were extirpated in the UK by game keepers. Falconers released new stock from Germany and Finland. This close to London, it's probably an escaped falconry bird."

"Have you hunted with goshawks?" the driver asked.

"Yes, many years." Vel didn't say when or how many years. Lines from Shakespeare popped into Tavistock's mind: *If I prove her haggard, though her jessies be my dear heart strings, I'll fly her against the wind to prey at fortune.*

The orderly asked, "Were you one of the falconry people who released the birds?"

Vel said, "Yes."

Tavistock suspected that Vel had gone back in time for some of the birds he'd released.

Vel said, "Letting the birds go can be hard. They're safer in falconers' hands. But then they'd be even safer if they didn't hunt. But they wouldn't be goshawks if you fed them like meat-eating parrots." He looked directly into Tavistock's eyes. "The goshawks found us and taught us to help them hunt. We only captured them later."

"Hawk gear probably wouldn't survive as relics past maybe 4,000 years in desert conditions," Tavistock said. "Most of what we have from before about 4,000 years ago is solid stuff—bone, stone, shell, antlers."

"Drawings," Vel said. "Paintings."

"Almost none in the UK. We need to get back in the car." The driver had already gotten into the car, and the orderly was closing in on Vel's elbow.

Vel moved before the other man's hand reached his elbow. "Robin Hood Cave, the ibexes," he said. "After I returned following one of the ice's advances and retreats."

The driver checked the GPS device to make sure it was working. "Off in the ass-end of Somerset," he said.

Vel leaned back. The hospital had given him a pillow to hold against the incisions if he felt uncomfortable, but he put it behind his head, then adjusted it until he looked comfortable enough and drifted off into a half-sleep, blinking slower and slower, head lolling and jerking him back awake.

Tavistock said, "We could call for a van with a comfortable gurney."

Vel said, "There is no such thing as a comfortable gurney. Could you just slide the seat forward a bit?"

The driver said, "Joe, if you got in front, he'd have more room." Tavistock nodded; the driver stopped on the verge, and Tavistock moved to sit beside the driver. Vel put the pillow against the car door and curled up away from the orderly who shifted his legs toward the other car door. He fell asleep like some wild thing retreating from capture the only way he could. Tavistock turned the radio on, volume low. It softly babbled about football and the housing market. Vel appeared to sleep on.

The car began passing groves of apples with apple harvest trailers parked between the rows of trees bent with ripening fruit. Vel took a deep breath, and said, "Apples. I won't miss Yule." He sat up in the seat. Ripe apples apparently oriented him in cyclical time.

The house looked the same—squat wide tower on the side of a larger ground floor building, the older great hall behind that. Vel said, "Go in the kitchen entrance, the ground floor here, not the hall."

The car stopped. Vel got out of the car, stiff and wincing, but he waved off the orderly. Tavistock asked the driver and orderly to wait with the car.

The driver said, "I've driven here before. Woman with MI5. It's an old Somerset family with an uncle who moved to Eastern Europe."

"That's me," Vel said, walking on ahead as he spoke.

Tavistock said, "We know about the MI5 woman." That she hadn't hidden the connection should be an ameliorating factor for her case.

Vel waited for Tavistock to join him at the kitchen door. Tavistock walked up, the driver and orderly stayed back. Tavistock heard two male voices on the other side of the door, then one of two middle-aged men opened the door. Both were trim, vaguely owlish, with short hair and somewhat broad faces. They looked like kin but didn't have Vel's long-legged leanness.

Vel said, "Joseph Tavistock. My kinsmen, Andrew Simmons and Darrell Evelyn. They're fourth cousins some generations removed. Met at one of my Yules—and they know my history."

Tavistock realized the two men were lovers, and Vel's explanation was to assure Tavistock that even the gay couples in the family observed the rules of consanguinity. They moved back from the door to let Vel and Tavistock in. The kitchen was one large room, dining area to the right of the door with a door to the ground floor bedroom beyond that, a central hearth that must have also heated the tower rooms from the chimney, and a dark green Aga to the left of that, with a couch and stuffed chairs and a smaller table to the left of the Aga, with a door on the far wall just beyond the Aga. The walls were white distemper and the floor was stone flag, but somewhat warm under foot. Tavistock realized that sometime after the house was built, someone had installed radiant sub-floor heating. A few paintings on the wall looked like museum replicas of arts from various eras. Tavistock looked at the art on the walls as the two men cautiously embraced Vel.

The younger man, Andrew Simmons, said, "It's always good to see you, Vel. We do wish the circumstances were better."

Darrell said, "So, you're Vel's keeper?"

Tavistock looked back from the walls and said, "One of them." He felt slightly mean and out of place.

Vel spotted the couch beyond the Aga and lay down on it, dangling his shod feet off the edge. "I'd be fine here and you could keep your room."

"We've been using the two tower rooms as offices, but we've got all that in one room. The other works fine as our bedroom."

Vel sat up and said, "I'd like it better if we were all on the same floor at night. Humor me. I heard you fixed the toilet in the kitchen bathroom."

"And we added a bath in the bedroom, which is why we thought that would suit you," Darrell said. "We'll get you a better bed in here."

Vel said, "I need a clean nightshirt. The orderly wrapped my suits in the ones I had and put them in the car boot. Andrew, can you get them in? Tavistock has some things to explain to you. I just want to sleep."

Tavistock fished out a pocket portfolio and unfolded the legal and medical directives. "It's written down here, and I'll leave the papers. He stays on the farm or on the road to the village stores except for medical emergencies or trips out with us. When he walks to the village, he needs to let the on-duty officer know when he leaves and when he returns. He needs to walk as much as he can tolerate. His lawyers are negotiating for more freedom and if this changes, they'll let you know."

Andrew came back with Vel's clothes and took them up to the tower rooms, returning with a clean nightshirt. Vel took it, slipped off his shoes, and went into the bathroom to change. When he came out, he sat on the couch to pull off his socks and dusted his feet against each other before swinging them up on the couch. Tavistock said, "I'll be back to have him show me his memory hoard."

Darrell said, "Bastard."

Vel said, "He'd wonder what I was hiding from him if I don't let him in. And he's just curious."

"It's really an imposition," Darrell said. Andrew nodded and went into the back bedroom to get a blanket for Vel.

Tavistock said, "Now, the medical restrictions," and read those out as Vel lay down on the bed, covered himself with the blanket, and put his forearm over his eyes.

Not lifting his arms from his eyes, Vel said, "No anal for six months?"

"Vel, please," Andrew said.

"I'll be here for Yule. No stairs, no heavy lifting. That probably means I can't make the fire. But I always make the fire." He sounded close to tears.

Tavistock wondered what making the fire entailed, but bid them good-bye and went back to the car for the return trip to London. None of them spoke much, the radio on, louder now, as a substitute for discussing anything. He didn't want to hear what Vel might have said after he left, sensing that Vel was on the verge of tears when he'd laid there with his forearm over his eyes. "Has anyone called to make sure the visiting nurse will be by daily to change the dressing?"

The orderly said, "Been done. Did you tell them to expect her?"

"Ah, shit. The family put me off again. His family takes advantage of him, and has been for thousands of years. And they think I'm the bastard, the cunts."

The orderly said, "Vel knows to expect the visiting nurse, so he won't be surprised."

The driver dropped the orderly off at a tube station and drove Tavistock all the way home. Isobel left him a note about taking Patrick out for dinner with friends from Wales and explaining there was a pie in the fridge he could reheat.

Apparently, the lawyers got Vel permission to work online. He ordered brain-tanned elk skins and deer sinew prepared for use as sewing thread from a US website after searching for UK sources of brain-tanned red stag skin. He also ordered parchment maker's tools, used to thin skins.

Tavistock wondered what that was about.

The team plus Peter Cooper sat around the conference table again the day before Vel's lover Emil was scheduled to land. Cooper opened the discussion. "After some debate, we've cleared the boyfriend to visit. Nobody can remember precisely why they thought it was a good idea to let him visit Vel in the hospital, though Quince appears to have been on the scene. The team that's investigating her now is being very careful to keep her beyond arm's length. So, there's a foreign national who knows what Vel is capable of, and we think his parents also know now. We could keep Vel close and happy, and Quince closer, or not. We went with making the man as happy as possible in custody since he was quite seriously wounded. Quince is the better prospect for us. She hasn't seen people hanged for their orientation, nor ever believed a priest who told her she had no soul. She's eager to serve her country for shit and giggles."

Tavistock thought that if Vel was the haggard hawk, then Quince was the brancher or eyas, screaming for attention. He also suspected that Cooper was bringing them decisions that Cooper himself had only a junior role in making. Cooper was forever quoting other people. Tavistock asked, "What color is Quince's hair this week?"

Dora said, "She's gone back to black."

Emil's visit was only eventful if one liked listening to other people's blowjobs without visuals, Tavistock thought as he listened to the tapes. Neither discussed Vel's situation, which was almost a statement in itself. They took walks as long as Vel was capable of taking, sat around playing music together on recorders and electronic piano. Emil cooked for Vel and taught him Slovak, which translated into innocuous enough things. They knew the house was bugged, that small drones carrying video cameras followed Vel's walks, and neither teased the listeners nor tried to evade them, unless the sex in the upstairs bedroom, now possible since Vel's visiting nurse said he could climb stairs, was teasing enough.

Tavistock didn't visit Somerset when Emil was there. Dora emailed:

> Using the electromagnetic signature off Vel's device, Marcus and I set up a couple of random scans near Bath and in London. Someone was wearing something like that. We found him, and he's being very cooperative, just pissed that Vel gave the game up. The device on Vel's ankle is the invention of one of his family members who has foreseeing but who is short-lived. We're working on his schematics, but I don't know who to test it on. He kept seeing events in his life that looked lethal and didn't have time enough to figure out how to dodge all of them, and suspected that one of them would get him and wanted the foresight to go away. Diana the Younger didn't want us to look for it in our present. Quince has lawyers keeping us from putting one on her. I'm still not sure they really work or if this device is a hoax, but Quince is being awfully fussy for a hoax.

He replied:

> So a goddess lied to us and it wasn't even a smart lie. I don't get the impression Diana is all that intelligent, despite the Columbia University position.

Tavistock hoped they could make a room-sized containment facility, a device for trapping gods. The family member who claimed to have invented it could be in on the ruse, though. Three weeks later, Dora emailed back to say that they'd got a working larger scale version set up to protect their studies of the smaller ones and discussions of the case. It caught Diana's fingernail as they turned it on.

Not magic, not a device that is invented because of the device showing up earlier than its invention in a weird time loop—a real thing that used batteries or mains current. Tavistock realized he didn't know when the batteries would run out on Vel's device. Quince's lawyers contested the use of a sub-contractor team to interrogate her, asking to have all interrogations take place with a full government agency, but hadn't tried to contest Tavistock's group's work with Vel.

Tavistock drove down to Somerset the day after he got Dora's email. Vel said, "Do you want the tour of the memory hoard now?"

"A good place to start." He didn't tell Vel about finding the device's inventor. Vel pulled a key ring from a peg near the kitchen door. Tavistock noticed that one of the keys was for a deadbolt lock and another was a high security key with encryption. Vel had upped his own security after Quince and Tavistock had met in one of the barns. Neither was supposed to have been there, Tavistock guessed. Or both were, but no more.

"Quince says that you found the person who invented this thing on my ankle," Vel said as they walked to the barns. "My family tends to produce quite sharp people."

Tavistock shrugged. They'd tried to put one on Quince; obviously that would get back to Daddy. "I never was sure the whole thing wasn't a trick on your part. One of your family seems to have invented it to keep from bumping into the ways he could die. Also, we don't know if it really works."

"Sight's useless for the short-lived. We have a longer time to change directions, to avoid the bad possibilities. For the short-lived, it's like being born in a car going 100 miles an hour into a stone bridge a mile away. Can't grow up fast enough to grab the wheel. I can figure out how to dodge things that look like they may be lethal coming from a couple hundred years out. Maybe all except the one that will kill me."

Vel opened a simple farm barn door to get to the inner doors with the very noticeable locks. Tavistock asked, "When did you put in these locks?"

"After Quince gave you the pot. I didn't want people stealing more of my memories. Don't move anything. They're in order." Vel turned on lights and Tavistock realized they were in a different barn than the one he'd been in. All the things in this barn were later than the Paleolithic and Neolithic. "Last 5,000 years," Vel said, "starting with some metal working equipment and ax molds. Roman slave chain about halfway up. Last two hundred years is a bit crowded, don't know what I'll remember or not yet from the recent past." He had a full lantern show set up, an early radio, an earlier movie projector, arc-lights, a Rolleiflex camera, a Nikon D300, and a sousaphone among other things that Tavistock wasn't taking in as separate objects. Then he spotted a British made Sinclair computer sitting by a big purple and gray enterprise Sun computer on casters. Wonderful toys. Vel picked up a telegraph key and balanced it on his hand just under his eyes, then put it back in the display case. "Clever people, clever people. Do you trust the thing on my ankle works now?"

"Dora said when they turned on the larger version, they clipped someone's fingernail. Turned out to be your cousin Diana the Younger. She lied to us."

"I wasn't sure you really believed any of us. You can't get inside our heads and see what we see with and without the device." Vel stopped talking for a moment, then said, "These things help me remember, but if I can't attach a story to something, out it goes to the shops. Unless it's bright and shiny on its own account."

Tavistock spotted a leather clubbing jacket toward the end of the last cases. Beside it was a large ball jointed doll that looked like a younger version of Thomas, Vel's ex.

"He really wanted me to remember him. I suspect that I will. I don't remember anyone ever leaving me before."

"So, most of the things in the barns are connected to stories?"

"Some things I keep at the house because they're connected to lots of stories that I like living with. I made some wolf-head beads out of amber, maybe after two generations of short-lived people died on me. People would steal them from me; I'd get them back. I still have them, except for the bead Quince stole from the necklace and doesn't think I'd miss."

Tavistock looked to see if Vel had any artifacts of him at the current end of the room. He saw the hospital pillow.

Vel said, "I'd like the device when you take it off of me."

Tavistock said, "What makes you think we'll ever take the device off in my lifetime?" Vel seemed less like a contemporary human in this space, more alien, though not particularly god-like as Tavistock imagined ancient gods to be.

"I could cut my damn leg off and go hide somewhere to regrow the foot, which it would if I didn't burn the stump. I'm cooperating with you for a reason. I'm not sure you'd…."

Tavistock fugued out a bit. Vel was saying, "You weren't there for a while. It's a hard thing to wrap your head around. You barely believe I exist, and this is even weirder, I suppose. And I have an odd trust of you that doesn't make any sense unless you did help me, will help me."

"I must have fugued out. Not sure why."

"Damn, let me try again. What I did more than 12,000 years ago, that I can't remember a damn thing about and which I've had to reconstruct from photo traps and from what Quince and I can see of the future, is that a younger self, a past double, comes forward. I'm the prime, the one on the unfolding time track, and he set a time trap that got me. Or the whole of European history unravels and we have a new history, one where you don't exist. Like the slice of missing time you just experienced. You're probably descended from one of the family men post Younger Dryas. Can't trace those without paternal DNA, and the women married thousands of men over the centuries and the boy children left the family. The mothers wouldn't be kin necessarily."

Tavistock came back out on the other side of another blank spell. Vel said, "I'll show you another video. I'll put it on a thumb drive. Take it. Show it to your team."

"What did you tell me when I was blanked out?"

"Something you didn't agree to do. I need to get you to consider possibly doing it. You erased yourself."

"What? How could I erase myself?"

"No, video first, then explanation. But I want to look at a few things while we're here, just to remind myself of how fast things changed in the last three centuries."

"You're upset?"

"Just be quiet and let me play with my memories, okay?"

Tavistock and Vel walked back to a loom shuttle from early steam- or water-driven weaving days, then up to a photograph of a locomotive with a bearded Vel standing back by the first passenger car, then to a suit neatly folded. "Sewing machine and mechanical loom," Vel said. "My first suit made that way, 1850s." Then the telegraph key he'd picked up earlier, no explanation, but apparently later than the dated suit. Tavistock wondered if Vel had installed private telegraph lines between the London shop and the Somerset house. Next were a painting and a bottle that used to contain cocaine. Vel moved forward to daguerreotypes of two young men, one naked, neither of them him. After the daguerreotypes came a pair of shoes made of leather with sewn and nailed-on soles. The order was Vel's personal history, not the history of the invention of the various things. The twentieth century began with a tray of machine-gun bullets, then a cigarette lighter. Various cameras, including a screw-mount Leica with its frosted chrome, knobs, tiny film-clutch lever, and black vulcanite body, fit in between the first radios and a Rolodex. Tavistock would need a warrant to get the names on the Rolodex.

"They're all dead now," Vel said. "Nothing useful to you. Antique business. Don't catch your breath next time you see something you want to investigate."

A pair of ice skates. A carbon fiber fly rod and a Hardy Princess reel. Beside the reel, a turkey bone flute looked anachronistic. *Tell us some stories, Uncle Vel.* Tavistock tried to remember what reel Isobel had been casting with when he saw her standing in the chalk stream. Tonkin cane and a Hardy Princess reel older than this one?

Vel walked on and picked up the ball-jointed doll. He stroked the small face with his fingertips, lingering over the eyes and lips. "This scared Thomas badly. I never quite understood why."

Tavistock said, "You bought it to remember him by. Maybe that reminded him too much that he was going to die and you were going to live many years beyond that. And some people just find the ball-jointed dolls creepy—too realistic for such immobile faces."

Vel said, "Chances could have been that I died from the gun shot, and Quince would be trying to convince you of why you need to help my past variation. Thomas would have outlived me then."

"We can trap your past variant now."

"That may be useful at the end of his stay in the future, actually. Let's go see the next video." Vel had a computer set up in a stall at the end of the barn. They stood to watch the video. It was short.

The boy in the videos appeared to be more hurt when the men of the group were looking than when they weren't. Tavistock said, "Another dissembling god. He's not as hurt now as he was, but he's pretending that he is."

"I'd been sneaking some food to him when I was shot. Leaving it where he or one of his family who'd help him could find it."

"Oh."

"He jumps, did jump forward. Are you with me so far? If you don't help him, all the history you saw in my memory hoard disappears. Still with me?"

"I can't not help him then. It's a time-binding?"

"Actually, you can refuse to help him, and time unbinds. Different people settle the British Isles, other parts of Europe. History is reset."

"So what did I refuse to do when you explained this quicker?"

"You didn't want to do it. You'd have to send your wife and son away, or involve them. You'd have to help him survive the first night, and you'd have to not use your device to trap him when he steals food for the past. I'll pay for what he steals. I think we can even provision him without him noticing. Then, when the band reaches good game country, we'd have to trap him and spank him so that he doesn't come back. He needs an excuse not to come back that the group's leader will believe. Slightly frozen paintball pellets would work nicely and leave weird stains to show his band."

"If it happens, it has to happen in the way that you and Quince see it happening?"

"Precisely. And he has to go back to the past and live my life as it was for the next 12,000 years."

"Time-trap?"

"Yeah, big-time time-trap. I don't go forward as much as I used to so that shit like this doesn't happen to my future selves, but for him, this is a matter of life and death."

"Not for us?"

"Non-existence didn't hurt, did it?"

Tavistock shuddered. Blank, non-time. "And you?"

"Whole Younger Dryas is blank time for me, but I do exist now. Or I think I do."

They started walking back toward the door, past all the objects Vel attached to memories.

Young and dressed in a coarse gray wool shift, Diana stepped from invisible past to now. "Why don't you just let the past go? What have you done in 14,000 years, Velius, and what has your family accomplished? They're just middle-class people living obscurely in decent comfort, sometimes when people around them died of starvation. Roll the dice again. Nothing could be worse than the twentieth century was."

Vel stopped. Tavistock wished he could take the anklet off Vel and put it on Diana, but she probably could evade him. Of course, she could evade him. Or rip his brains out.

She came up to Vel and put her fingers to his head again. "With that thing on you, I can't rip you apart or stuff you with thoughts, so I'll say this in words. All you have ever done is exist. You've never made great music, great art, or invented anything—that thing on your ankle came from one of your kin who hated his genetic heritage. You're not necessary to European civilization. Neither is your family. And European civilization isn't necessary to the human universe."

Vel said, "Things can be worse."

"My mother couldn't jump. She died in a concentration camp. The Nazis thought she was a gypsy, no papers. She saved a handful of short-lived people, is all. Great Diana of the Ephesians strangled in a concentration camp noose."

Vel didn't say anything for a moment. Tavistock couldn't think of anything worth saying. Then Vel said, "She died to protect some of the short-lived? I hope I've got the grace to do that if my time comes to that."

"They're all dead anyway. Or will be soon. And their old ages are so often very painful."

Vel said, "When were you born? And where?"

"Ukraine, 1928."

Vel said, "You're not that old then. That was a particularly bad period. You were awfully young to be left on your own."

"I bet that really works on your daughter."

"What if changing the past stopped your existence?"

"I'd love not to have existed. Not to exist."

"It's not what you do; it's the pleasures you take, the taste of a ripe fig in the mouth, the smell of an orchid, silk on the skin, meals with people you love."

"It's having to sleep wondering if people will find out and hurt you. I had to steal to survive. And that's what you're plotting, isn't it. I know what having to steal to survive is like."

"My double will think he's stealing. I'll be paying for it. You can change the future as well as the past. It's really easier. When are you coming from?"

"No, I won't say. You'll tell me it will be better later."

"You're not the prime. I think you're early. Soviet troops all over?"

Tavistock realized the Dianas they saw weren't necessarily in order. This one was the angry daughter who just lost her mother to the Nazis and saw Berlin raped by Russian soldiers. Another could be a future Diana who knew how things had gone but thought she'd slow them down by not telling them who invented the device on Vel's ankle.

Tavistock asked, "Can you see becoming non-existent?"

The Diana looked at him as though he was a yappy dog.

Then Tavistock's phone rang. Simon was on the line. "Quince accepted the anklet. Her mother overruled the lawyers."

Tavistock said, "Did you threaten Quince again?"

"I just wanted to read her. Daddy can't see or be read. It's not just a jump block and a seeing block. It closes the mind."

Vel said, "My compliments to the shade of your mother for the choice she made. Pity you didn't learn more from her."

"Don't—"

"None of my kin have invented napalm or the hydrogen bomb, or television or penicillin or computer chips, or even washing machines, but they lived and live decent lives."

"Vel, you're a shopkeeper. Occasionally, you get up the nerve to kill someone who's killing your pet dying ones or who's trying to kill you, and then you feel guilty about it for centuries. It's just pathetic compared to being Great Diana of Ephesus."

"Christians ran her off, didn't they?"

The Diana stepped toward them, but vanished. A few moments later, she, now older, stepped back from the left, materializing through one of the display cases and breaking the edge of it. "Yes, that was one of my younger doubles. But I agree with her—roll the dice for Europe all over again, see if history is kinder. Why not? Tavistock, keep your moral scruples and let a thief die."

Tavistock said, "You've lied to us before. What if this is all bullshit?"

The Diana shrugged and stepped back away.

"She fucked with my display deliberately," Vel said. He pushed the shards aside and looked in the case.

"How did that work?

"We can carry things with us, to about nine inches or so from our bodies. She pulled the glass loose in the move. Stole my Leica, too. Nine inches will get you pretty far inside a human body."

Tavistock called Simon back and said, "Did we get that on tape?"

"Yeah, after a weird blank out. Does Vel want to make a police report on the stolen Leica?"

Tavistock said, "Put one of the containment devices around the room with the monitoring equipment and the conference room."

Simon said, "Dora already did it. We're working now on putting it over facilities that need critical security. Diana Younger, PhD, seems to have done this in a nanosecond of her time when she was in a toilet."

The group met again with Cooper after the conference room was secured. Tavistock said, "Listen to me without making up your mind one way or the other, and don't dismiss this idea out of hand or we'll never get anywhere."

Cooper said, "We heard the tapes, though we're not sure why some parts appeared to be erased in the first hearing and then we could hear them when we replayed them. And we've got the second video."

Dora said, "What he's asking is that we look the other way when an earlier version of him comes up time to steal food for his people. So, either we do it, and make sure current Vel pays and that we can scare the earlier Vel straight after the crisis is over, or we don't and all the people kin to him, male side as well as female, disappear. We won't know they're gone. We won't know if we're gone. People have been calling doctors all over London reporting strange blackouts. Not that the doctors haven't also experienced it. Joe's experienced it. I've experienced it. If you let Vel's family of 12,000 years ago die, you won't even know we were ever here."

Cooper said, "I'm also one of those. We can't all be his family."

"The males had other families later. Not traceable except through father lines. Plus the descendants of anyone they helped survive at any time in history between the Younger Dryas and now would also disappear."

Simon said, "But we are here now."

Tavistock said, "Yes. I think that means we will, did, help him."

Marcus said, "What's the right tense for this?"

"We helped him. It hasn't happened yet for us. It's 12,000 years ago for him."

Lisa stopped taking notes and sat looking at the paper as though the ink had turned into living worms. "Why don't we just give him food to take back?"

Tavistock said, "Apparently that's not what happened, though we can shape the thefts a bit, show him something that he'll steal that was Vel's in the first place." He paused before he said, "Vel wants off his leash. He needs to collect anachronistic packaging and he wants to set up more remote cameras. He almost died. He wants to know what happened."

Cooper asked, "He doesn't remember?

"He says not."

Simon said, "We'd be cooperating with a thief."

Dora said, "Or he was cooperated with already, 12,000 years ago. The reset of European history—is it anything we'd really want?"

Marcus said, "It feels like a choice, but it really isn't, is it?"

Cooper said, "What would have happened if he'd died from the gun shot?"

Tavistock said, "Quince would have taken over. She'd have brought the younger Vel to me, apparently. I'd rather work with him than his daughter."

Cooper said, "The younger Vel could be caught by the shop owners, even shot. And how many people is he provisioning again?"

Tavistock said, "About sixteen, a little more than half women and children."

Cooper asked, "And that becomes what part of the UK population now?"

Tavistock said, "Apparently close to half in the south. Fewer in Scotland. A big chunk of the US goes away, part of South America. France is reporting blackouts, too, and there's some disturbance in Africa, tribal people in Dahomey who appear to be descended in part from people who came back from Europe."

Dora added, "I suspect that more people are blacking out but not taking it as significant."

Cooper said, "I understand that three-quarters of the women in the UK show early British settlement Paleolithic mother lines dating back to the last of the ice. A quarter of the men. Remember the man in Cheddar Gorge who proved to be related to a 9,000-year-old corpse found in a cave 300 yards from his home. Whatever. We don't really have a decision to make unless we think whatever population took these people's place would be nicer. I think we've become a sensible people. Our government paid reparations to the people held at Guantanamo when the Americans accepted lies against them. We cooperate with this younger Vel, and we get the UK we have now, or we don't and maybe it's a better world and maybe it's a worse world—if this isn't utter bullshit or a deeper game than we mere humans can understand."

Quoting again, Tavistock thought. He replied, "Already happened in the past except the emotionality of it that we have to live through, as Vel said."

Cooper jotted down some notes, probably what he'd quote back to his supervisors, then looked at Tavistock directly. "You'll keep the younger version of him at your house?"

"I'd be sending my wife and son on a holiday without me."

Simon asked, "When does all this happen?"

"We find him in early January. Quince can pin it down better. At least Vel thinks that's when we find him. Outside a gay bar."

"Trail of blood leading out of a toilet again?" Cooper asked.

"He's going to be hurt, but not in danger of dying, Vel said."

Simon said, "He could be testing our defenses."

"His family gave us what defenses we have against time-jumpers," Tavistock said. "We'll trap him and spank him when time comes to stop provisioning them. Vel

Prime disappears if Vel Double decides that here is preferable to the Younger Dryas."

Lisa, still with her pen off the paper, said, "We're still here."

Tavistock said, "So we help him provision this late Paleolithic band until they reach a place in the south with game and not too many other humans. Then we trap him, shift him out of his anachronistic blue jeans and tee-shirt, put him in garb Vel's making now with the hides and deer sinew off eBay, and scare him and shoot him on the arse with paintballs just as he's jumping so he doesn't come back."

Simon said, "All our meat. I'd come back. What's a paintball or two in the arse for a couple of tons of meat? Vel's script, and we're just going to walk through it. What are we getting from this?"

"Quince is going to try to explain things to the younger Vel. She can reach him despite the gap in languages. But we've also got to give him an excuse for the band. They'll want him to get meat the easy way. This will be his excuse not to go back."

Cooper said, "Quince is only wearing her device at night, but carrying it with her to use if she sees anything in her possible futures that scares her. We did a test with her wearing the device. Appears to work, unless she's a very good actress. I've got to kick this upstairs. We'll give you a decision later."

Simon said, "I think we should just make him an Eastern European problem. Tell them."

Tavistock said, "If you want to meet him, he's going to be throwing a Yule party. His lover and his lover's parents are flying in for the festivities."

"We could stop that, too," Simon said. "Let Europe re-set."

Tavistock said, "He's as much trapped in this as we are. And the stakes for him are much higher."

Simon said, "His family pimped him out and he wants to save them? And us to help him save them?"

Tavistock looked at Cooper, whose eyes wouldn't meet his. So Simon was taking the bad cop role, but this was coming from above. "It's so much more complicated than that."

Simon said, "No, it's simple. He's been alive for 14,000 years. He's nothing more than an antique dealer."

"No, I'm asking this group to help some of our starving ancestors."

Cooper interrupted. "We'll let you know."

Tavistock hugged Isobel and Patrick before he left, telling them he'd be back for Christmas. Yule, Winter Solstice, was a few days before Christmas.

He had moments of feeling insubstantial on the train going to Somerset. Cooper called to say that the people one level up and more were putting the decision back to the group since it had more experience working with Vel. Tavistock knew this meant that the group would be responsible if the thing failed or blew up in their faces and the high-ups hadn't accepted how big the blow up could be, or Cooper hadn't told them. Cooper had said that they'd come up with a decision by Yule or the day after. Tavistock said he wanted to help Vel. He'd come to trust him.

Vel, in an Austin Mini Cooper some years old, picked Tavistock up at the station. "I thought this would be better than having you have to rely on a cab being here. I've never seen the past shift the present so drastically. This is different."

Tavistock said, "I felt like a ghost on the train for a few moments."

Vel said, "So what's happening with the decision?

"They turned it back over to my team. So if you screw up, if we screw up, and someone at my boss's level knows, my team is expendable."

"If we screw up, the social fabric of the UK won't be around to punish you."

Tavistock asked, "What if we all didn't happen and something better happened?"

"What if it's worse? Two sets of people had to cooperate for this to work, and the initial conditions, as you saw in the video, were crap. Not that you trust me completely even now."

"I voted for helping you. How are you holding up?"

"Better enough. Quince is going to start the Yule fire, though. My family thinks I'm insane to have in-laws in on the family secret. But I haven't had in-laws in thousands of years. They've arrived, solid enough, not flickering, not noticing other people flickering."

"How do you like your in-laws?"

Vel turned down toward the small intersection with the shop and petrol station before answering, not that the empty roads demanded his attention. "Mother-in-law is wonderful. If I got sick like most people, I'd want her soothing me and making chicken soup. Father-in-law wishes I were a woman. I settled their old house and three acres on them. Emil accused us of haggling over him like a couple of old-fashioned patriarchs." Vel laughed. "We *were* two old-fashioned patriarchs haggling over him."

"You told them."

"You know I told them. Mom-in-law was not surprised. Father-in-law still wishes I were a woman. That's been a wee bit unpleasant."

"We're not really happy about having foreign nationals know."

Vel shrugged. "I wasn't going to let them think they'd really lost a son-in-law when I transition to a new passport. Assuming we have this future to come. If I didn't believe the future-to-come brings resolution with your people, a life with Emil, my mammoth farm with a nuclear power generator to get us through the next cold, I'd be very depressed." As the car got closer to the house, the traffic picked up, Vel's kin coming to celebrate Yule with him. Tavistock felt ghost-like. Vel said, "No decision yet."

"They said Yule or the day after."

"Been nicer to go into Yule knowing I'd have help." They could see Vel's house now and the cars parked around it.

"Is Quince watching for you? She's taken her anklet off."

"She finds the whole thing exciting." Vel pulled the car around to the side of the other parked cars. "Being young and invulnerable, and saving Great Britain as we know it, and not in love with anyone who can fade away makes life exciting. One of your bastards poked her with a needle to test the device and even that didn't bother her that much."

As Tavistock opened the passenger door, he said to Vel, "She's all future and no past."

Vel grimaced, slightly, as he opened his door. Tavistock didn't know if it was the injury or emotional. Vel put his feet on the ground and used the wheel and the side of the door to lever himself up. "If all this works out. She's flickered. Like you, she knows what that means and doesn't think it's just a slip of her mind."

"They're not sure they want to take the device off, and they're really sure they don't know if they want you going back to Eastern Europe."

"I need the device off, and I need to stay away from England when the double is here." They'd reached the door. Tavistock wondered if the team felt themselves flickering. Simon might see the flickering as a threat, some trick, and oppose Vel's request. Vel said, "Enough for now," as he opened the door and began smiling at his family.

For most of Vel's kin, Yule was the family event before Christmas with the spouse's family. They didn't all know what Vel was, but he was Uncle Vel, whether they were in on his secret or not. Tavistock had expected feyness, eccentricities, something other than the rather solid British people who cleaned the old hall, brought in camp beds and bedding, and took down the trestle legs and table tops from the walls to wash. The children ran out to see the ponies. Nobody appeared to notice the gaps of not being.

At about two o'clock, Vel, Emil, and Emil's father took a long walk in the countryside. Tavistock decided to leave them alone for that and went back into the kitchen. Quince was setting up two pieces of wood that would be the fire plow and furrow and looked determined to make this work. Emil came back alone. Vel and his father would spend the rest of the walk working with Vel's Slovak and looking at apple trees and farm machines. Despite minimal language in common, they shared a keen interest in farming. Emil seemed a bit put out to be reduced from Médecins Sans Frontières Doctor Hero to the son waiting for his beloved to come back from a long discussion with his father.

Emil said, "They're both landsmen, my father said. Only where Vel was born and grew up is under the North Sea. Even the land dies."

Quince said, "My dad gave your father his house back because it was full of ghosts that didn't belong to us. I think he was being metaphorical."

Tavistock left Emil and Quince and walked around looking at the new arrivals, overhearing conversations. None of the family appeared to be really rich, but were doctors, lawyers, various bureaucrats, shop owners. None were really poor either, but were skilled craftsmen, a plumber or two, couple of Corgi gas fitters. Several of them Tavistock recognized from Linux conventions. The family was free of snobbery over what family members did, apparently. A high percentage was gay, but apparently nobody else cared. The women were brisk with their children; the men doting.

Finally they'd finished washing the flagstones in the great hall before setting up the beds. Vel came back with Emil's father. They were both walking more alike, countrymen. Or Vel was being part chameleon. The sun was setting on the shortest day of the year.

Vel and some of the older children brought stone lamps from the cellar and put warm liquid fat in each. Quince showed Tavistock how to make juniper wicks by rolling the bark between his hands until it made a rough string. Each lamp got a wick. The children who could hold a lamp safely got one each, unlit. Vel checked with Quince to make sure she'd prepared the tinder correctly, dry as dust.

As the sunlight faded and the room darkened, Quince, barefooted in tee-shirt and jeans, knelt on the floor by the fire plow and began quickly rubbing the thinner stick against the grooved log. She moved to straddle the log, one leg bent, one leg extended to brace the log. Quince looked as though her honor depended on getting the flame going. Her face went slightly red. Vel bent down and began fanning the tinder gently. He smiled back at her and brought up a glowing coal in a mass of tinder that he juggled carefully in his hands, blowing gently at first, then harder. When the tinder burst into flames, he dropped it into a brazier full of dry shavings and began feeding it matchstick-thin kindling, then larger pieces of wood. He used a longer piece of thin wood to light one of the lamps. Quince stood up from the fire plow, pushed the grooved log into the fireplace, and tossed the friction stick in after.

Vel handed thin slivers of wood to the children and the lit lamp to the oldest girl. She passed the flame to the boy on her right, and he used his sliver of wood to light his lamp and pass the flame on to the next child. Soon the children were passing the flames more at random. By the time all the lights were lit, Quince had kindled a fire in the kitchen hearth. Vel took the children holding stone lamps to the hall where the big roasts and the Yule log waited. Tavistock gathered he shouldn't inquire too closely about the meat they'd be eating. Eating horse was illegal in the UK, but he wasn't connected to any agency that enforced that law.

People began drinking. Vel looked at Tavistock—had his group made its decision yet?

The whole group flickered. Vel looked at Emil, and the two of them showed Emil's parents from the bedroom behind the kitchen to the great hall. Vel was well enough to climb stairs, so he and Emil would take one of the tower bedrooms, and the older male couple who'd been tending Vel and the house would be in the other. Tavistock didn't know if he'd be staying the night or not, but Vel said the bed in the kitchen, while narrow, was comfortable and they'd surely have a nightshirt that would fit him. Tavistock felt that Vel was being awfully nice to what must seem to him to be his parole officer.

Emil took Tavistock aside and said, "He doesn't deserve to be bullied."

"It's not up to me at this point." Tavistock didn't know if Emil knew about the earlier Vel from the Younger Dryas who'd come, or who would be coming, to steal meat to feed his people and the men who apparently were holding them captive. Tavistock didn't think those people in the past particularly deserved to live, but if they were to live, they had to move south, not wait for the weather to improve. It wouldn't improve for some thousand years. Tavistock asked Emil, "How is your family taking this?"

"Far better than I'd expected. Vel is charming, of course."

"Where did you meet Vel?"

Emil didn't answer for a second, half-turned away from Tavistock, and poured himself a coffee from a pot on the Aga. He said, "We're announcing our union tonight, regardless of what you do to Vel."

Tavistock said, "His last partner dissolved their union to take up with someone else."

"Thomas found out he could love old men. He had wondered how Vel could." Emil sipped the coffee, then continued, "I met Vel in a Bratislava gay club, but I'd seen him earlier. He bought state land that had been confiscated from my family."

Tavistock thought, but didn't say, so Emil whored the land and house back.

Quince came in and said, "Things are chaotic tonight. I see too much and too little. Vel would like to be off his control device, but not at the risk of the house and family." Tavistock had hoped the family could push back more than his team realized, but knew that that strength might make them seem like a threat. Quince said to the group, "Come to the hall. Everyone's dancing."

In the hall, people had moved the beds against the wall and brought in a stage and generator for the loudspeakers. The roasts in the giant hearth smelled wonderful. One was a whole pig, the others were two hind legs that Tavistock wouldn't ask questions about.

Vel and Emil began dancing together. They stripped down to briefs and sweaty skin. Vel still had his awful scar running down his belly, and the exit wound was like a crater in the small of his back. Carolyn, dancing alone, watched him closely. The two men stopped dancing and wrapped their arms around each other to announce their upcoming union. Tavistock hoped this could happen as they planned.

After hearing the congratulations from the group flickering in the firelight and possibilities, Vel and Emil toweled off and put their clothes back on before walking outside. Carolyn stopped Tavistock from following. Quince came up behind them and asked, "Where are your wife and son?"

Tavistock turned to look directly at her, and she looked hard into his eyes. If she could see all possibilities, she knew what Tavistock's wife was, whether his suspicions were fantasies born from his contact with Vel or hard truth with an ending she could see and wouldn't tell him. Tavistock said, "My wife doesn't like large crowds, and my son is only four, a bit too young for all this."

"We put the children to bed in the hall and move the party to the barns and other places," Carolyn said. "They enjoy playing together."

Quince said, "I can't see his wife."

Tavistock said, "Perhaps I should get a room nearby, see you in the morning if someone could call me a taxi or drive me to a motel or hotel."

"Stay the night," Carolyn said. "You're going to be tapped for Vel's midnight ceremony. Also a woman who is family who works for MI5, and her boss, and the in-laws."

Quince said, "He'll stay the night, but his group went home without making a commitment to help us."

But Tavistock hadn't seen flickering in the last hour, which he thought was a good sign. He said, "I'm sorry it's still hanging. I probably should have stayed in London to try to convince them."

"Vel's drinking a bit more than usual. Can you try to—"

"Maybe the poor bastard needs to get drunk."

When Vel and Emil came back, some of the younger gay men of the family began arguing with him. "You obviously could have taken some of us with you. It's not like we don't know about bigotry here."

Vel said, "I'm sorry. Some of you could join us in May."

"You can bring some of us now."

"I've got to see what happens in the next couple of months," Vel said. Again, Tavistock thought that he liked Vel but wasn't too fond of some of the family.

One of the younger men said, "I suppose you're exclusive with that one."

Vel said, "I don't sleep with men whose diapers I've changed."

"You never changed my diapers," the younger man said. "My mom ran away from this crazy family."

Emil moved closer to Vel. His father scowled. Emil's mother touched her husband on the shoulder. Tavistock saw that all of them had glasses in their hands full of the potent Somerset apple brandy, but Emil seemed less drunk than the rest. Tavistock hadn't been drinking at all.

The young man said, "You just left us here. I can see why my mother fled to the United States. This family pretends to be this sexual Brigadoon, separate from the rest of the UK, but it's just free for you."

"That's not true," one of the two men who'd nursed Vel when he came out of the hospital said.

Vel said, "I know not to get involved with family men. I don't want to risk—"

"—tearing the family apart. But you did that when you fucked off to Bratislava and only came home when you got fucking shot."

"Glaciers," one of the other younger men said. "A fucking thousand or more years from now."

Tavistock wondered if the young man really wanted to sleep with Vel. Neither he nor Vel said anything that was other than cutting, but at least Vel was defending himself. He said, "Even if you weren't family, I'd stay away from you, bitch." *Um, defending himself like a drunk.*

Everyone shut up then. The boy who'd said Vel had never changed his diapers turned pale. Tavistock moved in to make sure he didn't hit Vel for that. Emil tried to pull Vel away.

Emil and Tavistock stood in front of Vel. The boy said, "I didn't deserve that."

Vel walked away into the dark. Emil's father nodded at his son, who followed Vel.

Tavistock told the boy, "It isn't really about you, tonight."

"Ah, the warden, the probation officer. Is Vel just fantasizing about going back to Bratislava with his doctor lover? That's a monitoring cuff on his ankle, isn't it?"

Flicker. One of the older men said, "I'm not quite sure why we're all so keyed up. Maybe tomorrow we'll take him and Emil clubbing." The group walked back into the house on the kitchen side. Tavistock waited for Vel and Emil to get back. They nodded at him and walked toward the great hall, with Tavistock following them. Vel said, "At midnight, I do a ritual for the people who know the history. I've got to go down under the house. The main entrance is through the kitchen, but I think I'll avoid that right now. There's another way. I need to go prepare."

Emil and Tavistock moved the rocks that usually blocked the second entrance. Vel put a small electric torch in his teeth, opened the small wooden hatch and went down the tunnel.

Tavistock asked, "Should he be going down there alone?"

Vel said from the hole, "Please don't follow me. You'll both come down through the kitchen stairs at midnight. Emil, bring your parents. Joe, get Quince and Carolyn. There's someone from MI5, the woman you asked me about and her boss. I thought I'd try to get her boss to understand."

Tavistock said, "You sure you're not overdoing things."

Vel said, "Stop worrying about me," and Tavistock heard his scrabbling down the tunnel fading.

At midnight, Tavistock heard strange flute music as he came down the kitchen stairs to the cellar. Behind a horned mask that left his lower face naked, Vel played on a bone flute. He was dressed in a loincloth and a leather shirt, barefooted on the cold floor. When everyone was in the cellar, he put the flute in his loincloth's waist band and said, "I've been alive for 14,000 years. Now my life is in your hands."

The woman from MI5 trembled. Her boss put his hand on her shoulder as Vel took off the mask. Tavistock noticed that the walls of the cellar were painted—Paleolithic animals, Roman horses and riders, a helicopter. The paintings looked new and ancient at the same time.

Vel moved through the group, kneeling before each person, joining hands. "Please remember that my life is in your hands. I'm not asking for secrecy if you have other loyalties."

When her turn came, the woman from MI5 took Vel's hands and nodded. Her boss did the same.

Vel said, "I can't swear you to secrecy since I've broken it myself."

Everyone flickered. Tavistock thought his team had gone home.

Tavistock was last to hold Vel's hands for the oath. Then Vel took off the skin shirt and pulled on a hoodie and sweat pants, bunching up the loincloth under the pants. He walked over to the MI5 woman's boss and said, "I don't know if I can convince you that I didn't ask her to get the job, but I didn't. I really...I don't want her to lose a job over me."

The man said, "Your family are all decent Englishmen. I'll see what I can do."

Vel said, "I should go to bed. Need to cheer the sun in with the kids." He seemed even drunker than he had during the confrontation with the young boy.

Emil stayed close to him as he walked with the group up the stairs. In the kitchen, some of the other people there looked at Vel and the rest of the group knowingly. Carolyn cleared the kitchen so Tavistock could sleep on Vel's kitchen bed. Emil said to Vel, "Are you sure you're okay?"

"Fine."

Carolyn brought Tavistock a nightshirt and asked, "Do you need anything?"

Tavistock decided to sleep in his clothes since he didn't know who'd be coming and going through the kitchen early in the morning. Emil's father and mother went into the back ground-floor bedroom.

After everyone else was out of the kitchen, Tavistock called the monitoring system to report what had happened that night. After that the man from MI5 came in and asked if they could talk. "Cooper said you've gotten to know Vel fairly well by now. Do you trust him?"

"I voted that we help him when his younger self comes up-time looking for food."

"The fugues are related to that?"

"Not helping him erases European history as we know it."

"And Quince, the girl who kindled the fire, is his daughter and wants to work for the Crown. Do you trust her?"

"Not as much as her father. She needs him to help her manage her talents. She's headstrong, but she hasn't been through what he's been through."

"I've seen the reports. You don't think he would have infiltrated us?"

"With Quince, he doesn't need to infiltrate us."

"Oh?"

"You haven't seen those reports? Contact telepath, major seer. Only thing she can't do is jump in time."

"No, I hadn't seen those reports, just his. Should you have told me about her? It's a hard decision. We still don't know whether this is a hoax or if he's really what he says he is. The device on his ankle could be allowing him to fake having talents he says he can't exercise now because of the device. He could be something completely alien, too."

"I believe he's what he says he is. My team's dealt with another one. They're not all friendly. Watch out for Diana the Younger."

"Was he drinking a lot tonight?"

"Yes. He's under several different kinds of stress, from the gay kids in the family for not taking them to Slovakia, from us for not making a decision to help him, and from meeting the in-laws and not really knowing how that's going to work out, or even if he can go back now that we've pulled his passport and keep him from jumping by holding his family hostage on top of whatever the device does. All of this is a huge change for him. Emil and he were being very brave about the betrothal. I suspect whatever happens, the old man gets his house back."

"There is physical evidence for the long life?"

"Yes." Tavistock was exhausted by now and just wanted to sleep. "Are you staying the night?"

"No, we're leaving. I'll talk to Cooper now that I've seen the family. I think they're worth saving. Girl's job, not. One spends one's political credit where it's important."

Tavistock said, "The changes would be far greater than the simple loss of the people who'd been at Vel's Yule this past day." The MI5 man looked like he wasn't really convinced the problem was that serious.

Vel and the children didn't wake Tavistock when they went out to greet the sun. What woke him was Vel and Emil talking about what Vel needed to take for his hangover and why he needed cufflinks and a suit to see his guests off. Tavistock looked at his watch. 11:30.

Emil fed Vel a glass of orange juice and two aspirins and said, "You need to get back to bed. And why does your suit jacket have working button holes in the sleeves?"

"Not yet. Real suit jackets have working button holes in the sleeves, supposed to."

Carolyn came in with Quince. They looked at Vel from across the kitchen. Quince said, "It's not just a hangover." Carolyn went out to her car and came back with a medical bag. She asked Vel, "What do you absolutely need to do today?"

"See my guests off."

"Emil, what did you give him?"

"Two aspirins and about 500 milliliters of orange juice. No coffee. You think he—"

"No coffee," Quince said.

Carolyn said, "Let's see the guests off."

"It was a crap Yule," Vel said. He felt his chin. "I don't remember shaving but I saw the sunrise with the children."

"When I woke up, you were shaving," Emil said. He, on the other hand, hadn't shaved.

Carolyn said, "Get his cufflinks done, Emil, then go shave while he's saying good bye to the family."

Vel said, "I thought the boys wanted to take me clubbing."

Carolyn said, "If you're awake at 10 tonight, and if you haven't overdone things, and if you're not worrying about—"

"I haven't had a hangover like this in centuries, I don't think."

"More than a hangover," Carolyn said. "Go say good bye to the guests, and then I'm going to look at your belly and probably sedate you. Just mildly, since you still have alcohol in your system."

Vel didn't bother to argue. Carolyn said, "Joe, you can use Vel's room tonight." She walked out with Vel to bid the guests good-bye.

Tavistock noticed that no one had flickered in a while and wondered who in his team had been the voice of compromise and reason. Quince said, "Answer your phone" about a half second before it rang. He'd picked it up to show her it wasn't ringing when it did. He walked outside the house to take the call, and saw Vel smiling at his departing guests out in the car park, head bobbing, tilted slightly to the side, gracious host under any conditions. Carolyn looked back at Tavistock.

Cooper was on the conference room speakerphone, with various bodies making noises in the background. "We want you to bring him in for a lie-detector test tomorrow. If that satisfies us, we're going to help him."

"What was the prevailing argument?"

"All contemporary humans are descended from people who did what they had to do to survive. Most of us now haven't a clue what crimes might have made our lives possible." Tavistock knew Cooper was quoting someone even higher up this time. Cooper continued, "We're helping some of our female ancestors. And we started to notice that we had fugue states when the other argument prevailed. And someone from MI5 called us to say that the family were fine British people and that he felt we should help. We don't know who would have populated the UK if it wasn't us, but we'd like it to be us."

"Not that you'd notice if you never existed," Tavistock said. "What can I tell Vel? He's having a combination of hangover and anxiety attack, plus he may have been overdoing it physically last night."

"If we're satisfied by the lie-detector test, we'll help him." Cooper disconnected without saying good-bye. Tavistock closed his phone and went back in the house.

Quince said, "Tell Dad 'if we're satisfied with the lie detector test, we'll help you.'"

"Yeah," Tavistock said. He didn't know if Quince overheard or just plucked the words from the most promising future.

Tavistock and Quince sat waiting for a few minutes. Emil finished shaving first and came back down. Tavistock said, "I have good enough news for Vel."

Emil said, "He can't help being who he is. Why not create a passport for him? I want him back."

"What has he told you about what it was like during the Younger Dryas?"

"Nothing."

"He or a double of him is coming forward from then, foraging for his family back then."

"Whoring for pizza? He jokes about having done that," Emil said.

"No. He's not going to be in shape for that."

Quince said, "He'll barely make the time-jump, but I don't see a future where he doesn't make it."

"You don't exist if he doesn't make it," Tavistock pointed out.

"Well, there is that."

Tavistock suspected that Quince told Carolyn about the phone call before he got it. Carolyn and Vel came back in from seeing the guests off, Vel quivering slightly.

Tavistock said, "If you pass a lie detector test and convince us that you're not going to take advantage of us, and that you're who and what you told us you were, we're going to help you.

Carolyn said, "Now, is there anything else you have to do today?"

Emil said, "Clubbing is out."

"I don't have to do anything more, then," Vel said.

"Joe, tell them I gave Vel half a dose of Valium at 12:39 p.m. I'll write it down, milligrams. If the examiner thinks it will interfere with the test, wait a day. Vel, take off the suit and whatever you're wearing for underwear." She handed him a linen nightshirt. Vel went into the bathroom to change and handed Emil the suit and shirt and a loincloth. The shirt fell to his calves. He sat down on the bed, one arm bracing him upright.

Carolyn said, "I need to check your belly. Pull the sheet up to your hips, then pull the shirt up to your rib cage and bend your knees." Vel lay down and complied. Carolyn felt carefully and asked Emil if he'd noticed any rectal bleeding.

Emil said he knew better than to do anal with Vel at this stage of recovery, and Carolyn looked at him and said, "What, no rimming?"

"No bleeding."

"Emil, we'll get you a mat so you can stay by Vel. Joe will take the bedroom you were in."

"I want to straighten up in our bedroom," Emil said.

Carolyn said, "Honey, nothing ever could straighten up that bedroom." She handed Vel a pill, then a glass of water. He took the pill, and then she walked back to her car with the medical bag. Tavistock followed her. She said, "People think, well, Vel has all the time in the world, so he needs to attend to our problems right now since we're not going to be around forever. Only his minutes aren't any longer than ours."

"He said."

"I like him very much even when he exasperates me, which he does from time to time in sometimes spectacular ways, and don't want him to die on my shift. I want to pass him on to the next generation."

Vel slept, oblivious to the family coming and going through the kitchen. But when the two men who lived in the house began to reheat slices of the roasts for dinner, he sat up and blinked. Vel's in-laws were out of their bedroom; Quince was setting the table. Tavistock felt like he was in the way.

Carolyn looked at Vel and asked, "You feel like joining us for dinner."

Quince said, "Yes."

In his nightshirt, Vel walked barefooted across the floor to the kitchen table and stood staring at it as if counting the seats.

Carolyn said, "Emil, you and your parents should sit here." She pointed to the head of the table. Tavistock sat down on a couch near the table, not sure he should eat with them or later. "Vel, sit by Emil. Tavistock, just sit somewhere."

Everyone ate without talking. Carolyn kept her eyes on Vel, who ate with his fingers, neatly rolling up a meat slice. After he'd eaten a couple slices of reheated roast and an apple, and drank more orange juice, Vel went to the bathroom, then lay down on the bed and went back to sleep. After cleaning up, all the people still at the house sat in the kitchen for a while watching telly, which didn't seem to bother Vel at all. At about 10 p.m., Tavistock went to Vel's tower bedroom.

He giggled when he saw it. Only major reconstruction could straighten out that bedroom and the adjoining bathroom. Over the bed was a fitting for either a trapeze bar or a sling. Both the trapeze and the sling hung on the wall by the window. Beside the bed were two large market baskets of sex toys that went far beyond what Isobel had, including a box of nitrile gloves and an unopened jar of Boy Butter. The bathroom had a piped-in anal douche with a basket of silicone fittings. Tavistock felt torn between giggling even more nervously and going downstairs to see about getting a cab to lodgings. He thought about adding to the official report that the subject was playful and imaginative as shown by his sex toys. Instead he called the after-hours number for his group and asked them to let him know where or if he should expect a driver. He pulled off his clothes and put on one of the ubiquitous linen nightshirts, then lay awake wondering how all this would play out.

Moments later, Tavistock got a call back telling him to expect a driver at 7 a.m. He set his watch alarm for 5:30. He could at least shower before putting his clothes back on.

By the time Tavistock got downstairs the next morning, Vel was dressed in the suit he'd worn when seeing his guests off, pacing in small circles on the stone floor. Carolyn and Emil were eating fried eggs and rashers of bacon. Going by the greasy plate left on the table, Vel had already eaten. Vel stopped pacing and picked his empty plate up and put it in the sink. Tavistock said, "A driver is coming for us at 7. Vel, are you ready?"

"I'm ready."

Carolyn wrote out what she'd given Vel last night on a slip of paper she handed over to Tavistock, who put it in his pocket. Tavistock asked, "Have you had a lie detector test before?"

"Not that I remember yet," Vel said, implying time loops Tavistock hadn't imagined.

The driver opened the doors to the back of the sedan, and Vel and Tavistock got in. The car didn't stop until it reached the safe house in the suburbs southwest of London. Vel asked if they were going to where Tavistock worked and Tavistock shook his head. The safe house wasn't a house per se, but a small office building.

"Nice not to have to go through London traffic," Vel said as the sedan pulled into the car park. Tavistock wondered who of his team would be in the observation room. They checked in at the front desk, and the receptionist directed them to a conference room behind two sets of locked doors that the driver opened for them.

The chair and apparatus were waiting, along with a burly man with short graying stubble on his round head and very blue eyes. He looked at Tavistock first and said, "I'm the examiner. Couple of your teammates have been helping me with the questions. I take it there's sufficient physical corroboration and a daughter with some impressive talents." He then turned his head and smiled, "You must be Vel, last name Parker."

"Velius, last name's kind tagged on to fit in."

"You must know how this works. It's the old fashioned polygraph with some additional reading of electrical activity in the brain and eye movements."

Vel nodded.

Tavistock said, "His family doctor said to tell you he'd had half a dose of Valium yesterday, if that would interfere." He handed the man Carolyn's note.

"Shouldn't. Velius…"

"Vel's fine. I can also answer to Bill or Will when I'm half asleep." Vel walked around the chair, touching the fittings gingerly.

"I understand you had abdominal surgery for gunshot about three months ago. If you need to take a break, let me know."

Vel nodded again. The examiner pointed to chairs at the table, and they sat talking inconsequentially about Vel's Yule celebration, the price of diesel fuel for tractors, and then Vel dropped out of the conversation when the examiner and Tavistock talked about football. The examiner noticed and tried ale breweries, and found out quite a bit about perry and local Somerset ales.

"Well, let's sit you down and put on the gear. Not claustrophobic? Should take about an hour for the first session. We'll break for lunch, then we'll have some new questions based on the results of the first session."

Vel moved to the chair with the lie-detector apparatus and stood beside it. He said, "Should I take off my jacket?"

"Yes, please, and pull your shirt tails out."

Vel looked at Tavistock and sighed, then flashed a little smile as he unbuttoned the jacket sleeves. He took the jacket off and handed it to Tavistock, who folded it, laid it over a chair, and found another chair to sit down in.

Vel sat down. The examiner stuck some electrodes on Vel's chest up under his shirt, then on Vel's head. Then he strapped the sweat detectors onto Vel's hands and put the chest expansion detector around his chest.

"Just sit there a moment while we get a baseline reading. We're also going to have a camera recording your eye blinks."

"Carolyn told me not to lie, even if the question was embarrassing or the answer might not be—"

"Quiet now."

Vel nodded and sat quietly. The examiner watched the readings for a while, then said, "We'd ask you when you were born, who your parents were, but I don't think those are neutral questions in your case."

"About 14,000 years ago, as far as I can tell," Vel said. "Somewhere that's under the North Sea now. My mother I remember quite well, I think, because I've told people stories about her over the years. I never knew who my father was."

"Okay. Why did you move to England?"

"Winter pasture for the horses and good hazel nut harvests."

"Present time, why here now?"

"Tavistock figured out what I was. I knew that he might help me."

"Who shot you?"

"Someone like me. Time-jumper. Who precisely, I don't know."

"You said you killed him in self-defense?"

"I think so. He hasn't come after me again."

"Where did this take place?"

"Probably Scotland, about 10,000 years ago. I jumped forward to the hospital before I bled out, before the pain took hold. He followed me back from more or less last year, I think."

"Why would another time-jumper want to kill you?"

"Because I wasn't going to hide anymore. I was going to need help from the short-lived. I wanted my family to survive the Younger Dryas, the ice returning. I didn't ask him why, really."

"Do you think you're a god?"

"Not as you today think of gods. Like in the Greek myths or Norse sagas. I'm long-lived, capable of what seems sort of like magic, probably isn't."

"Do you want to be worshiped?"

"No."

The examiner moved over to the recording instruments, then back to face Vel. "Bit of a reaction there."

Vel closed his eyes tightly. He opened them before he answered. "I had a very bad experience with being worshiped. Short-lived ones aren't all natural subs."

"What planet did you come from?"

Vel's eyes opened a bit wider. "This one. I can't see other planets."

"Seeing?"

"Before I step to another time and place, I have to see it."

"How much control do you have over time-jumping?"

"It's not like catching a bus. Some places I can see and can't go to. Time locks. I didn't happen then. Sometimes, I'm in the past and can't come home again until I do all the things I did. Futures may or may not materialize."

"We've put a device on you. Does it keep you from seeing or jumping?"

"Yes. I can't see the possible futures now. Can't jump. Also protects against contact telepathy."

"Do you resent us putting this on you?"

Vel hesitated, closed his eyes again, then said, eyes still closed, "Yes, even though I knew it was going to happen. But it was better than some of the other ways you could have kept me from seeing or jumping."

"Thank you. We can read the movements of your eyes behind closed lids, you know."

Vel opened his eyes. "That was one of the trick questions, wasn't it?"

The examiner shrugged, and moved back a bit from Vel. The examination continued with questions about Emil, Quince, the old policeman who'd been his domestic partner, and the incident in a brothel in Amsterdam that Tavistock had heard about.

Vel said, "I thought I'd understand death if I bled until I was unconscious. The incident insulted Thomas. He was right. The brothel's blade-scene spotters were going to step in even if I didn't use the safe word."

The examiner turned to lighter questions about the house and the memory hoard before stopping the examination by holding up his large meaty hand. Then the examiner unhooked Vel from the apparatus and said, "We'd like a demonstration of time-jumping."

Tavistock wasn't expecting this. He said, "Vel, would you fuck off to ancient China or someplace where we don't have jurisdiction if I take off the device?"

Vel paused before saying, "No."

The examiner said, "But you considered it?"

"Of course."

A young man pushed a trolley of pasties, sandwiches, and urns of coffee and tea into the room. "After lunch," the examiner said as he poured himself a cup of coffee from the urn.

Vel said, "Why not get it over with now?" The examiner nodded at Tavistock, who bent to Vel's ankle and unkeyed the device, hoping that it hadn't been booby-trapped. Vel didn't say anything. Tavistock had expected he'd say thanks.

Vel walked up to the trolley and poured a cup of coffee. "See? Hot." He looked intently into the air, then stepped into an invisible place. Tavistock had trouble breathing. Before the coffee in normal time could have cooled, Vel stepped back and handed the coffee cup to the examiner who touched the surface of the liquid with a finger.

"Well, you ruined a cup of hot coffee. Where did you go?"

"Oxford, after the invention of the Styrofoam cup. I love Oxford in the spring." Vel pulled a flyer for an anti-war march out of his pants pockets.

"Okay, you can time-jump. And there's physical evidence for really long life. Eat some lunch and we'll hit the second set of questions after that."

Tavistock said, "Should I put the device back on?"

Vel looked through the food on the cart and picked up a meat pie and an apple. He said, "You've got my family hostage, both here and in the Younger Dryas."

Tavistock pocketed the device. If they were going to work with Vel, he had to trust him. "I'm not your enemy, but the powers scare us."

"Your fear is scary for me. I don't want to be taken apart for parts or locked down for the rest of my life with that thing and put in a cell, or kept drugged or in pain for centuries. I've given you Quince. She comes with less baggage than I do, even if she's a bit of a brat now."

The examiner said, "I'm glad I don't make policy."

Vel said, "It's not really obvious what to do with me, is it?"

"You've got some impressive connections with that family of yours," Tavistock said.

"They pushed a bit too far, didn't they, and your team was ready to let their ancestors die off in the Younger Dryas," Vel said. "Put the device back on me before I start looking at the afternoon session."

"You're sure."

"Yes."

Tavistock put the device back around Vel's ankle and keyed it closed again. Vel said, "It's not that I can't guess where the afternoon session is going."

Vel struggled through questions about Quince, the woman in MI5, the connections to influential people through the antique trade. Vel told them who explicitly knew his secret before the recent Yule.

The examiner asked how he'd protected himself when family members rebelled against him.

Vel's voice went flat, and he admitted he'd put people in asylums. Good Old Uncle Vel. "Seems like a waste now. I got them out when I could, when they agreed to keep their mouths shut. Some of them were mad to begin with."

Tavistock thought about the boy who'd been furious about being refused by his *soi-disant* uncle. Vel continued, "When I could see a possible problem coming, I tried to get the parents to move. This has only been a problem over the last thousand years. Mostly over the last 500 years."

The examiner paused. He asked if Vel was tired or in pain at the moment.

"I'm tired," Vel said. "Not in pain."

"Okay. We'll get some tea." The examiner went to the back door, and the boy who'd served them lunch brought in a teapot in a cozy, some sliced oranges, and a cake. Vel drank his tea holding the Styrofoam cup with both hands. He kept blinking his eyes though Tavistock didn't see any tears.

"Stay with him, please," the examiner said to the tea boy. "Tavistock, I'd like to talk to you in private."

Tavistock followed the examiner through the room's back door, into a kitchen with a microwave, electric stove, and refrigerator. The examiner said, "The obviously safe thing would be to not trust him. He's trying to be ingratiating, but there's an undercurrent of something else, big distance. We're going to show him the two videos he gave you and see how he reacts to those."

Tavistock said, "I don't think anyone wants to make policy on this one. I don't want to see that first video again. Not since I've gotten to know him."

"Then stay in here. Higher-level thinking is that if he wanted to steal anything, not just food for those people, he could have just done it. Left it for them at night. Why involve us?"

Tavistock said, "Time-trap. It didn't happen that way. And if the boy he was doesn't supply the food, the band doesn't need the boy alive. They'd butcher the sick for meat."

"Neat camera he used. Automatic facial recognition. Could have zoomed in on a bit. He knows you've seen it. Might be good if you're in the room."

"Are you going to ask him questions?"

"We're just going to show him the videos, the one he sent you, the later one he showed you in his memory hoard. If they're fake, with actors, makeup for him, he's not going to show the same reaction as he would if that really happened to him. Unless he's a really good actor himself. Let's go back and get set up for the show."

The tea boy brought in a large flat screen monitor. Vel looked at the monitor, then at Tavistock, who realized Vel knew without sight what this would play, just as Tavistock knew without telepathy that Vel knew. Vel sat back in the examination chair without the examiner asking. He said, "Tavistock?"

"I didn't ask for this. I'll leave the room if you want."

Vel said, "No. Stay. You're going to be the one who takes in the double. Can we say 'him'? I know I was that person, even if I don't remember any of this."

"'He', then," Tavistock said.

"Anyway I can just be hooked up and just have Tavistock in here. You could give him your list of questions."

"I've seen it already," the examiner said.

"Okay," Vel said from his straps and monitoring devices. He sat for a while so the examiner could get his baseline again. Vel fidgeted. The examiner held his hand out at Vel, like a traffic cop's gesture to stop. Vel said, "Let's just get this over with."

"Okay." The examiner turned down the overhead lights. "We enhanced it a bit."

Vel flinched. The first video began, and Tavistock looked away from the screen at Vel who rolled his eyes toward Tavistock, then back at the screen.

A woman was arguing with a man.

Vel said, "The band leader wasn't that bad. The man who kept me in pain to control me was an uncle or a brother, I'm guessing."

On screen, Vel was bent over, blood coming down his side where so many centuries later a British surgeon removed a calcium nodule with a quartz arrowhead in it.

The examiner said, "You look younger."

"I'd gone through puberty again. Not my first. After a couple of puberties, you know that the emotionality is just temporary. But the hormones still make everything so dramatic. Your adult self scrabbled around in the back of your mind, trapped out of the decision process. Everything goes black and white and deadly serious again. Only, this time, it *was* all deadly serious."

The examiner briefly shone a torch on the charts moving under the pens.

The man who was keeping Vel in pain was also raping him. Tavistock knew that was coming up next and looked away. No soundtrack, for which he was grateful.

Vel said, "Yeah, that, too. And one of the little girls looks like she's dying. They'd be thinking about eating us. I'm not bringing them any luck. She's going to die anyway." The mother of the young dying girl looked at the flint knife. The man holding it pulled back. *Wait. See if our luck changes.*

Vel straddled a log and stared at the camera. Tavistock remembered that scene and looked back at the screen. Had the younger Vel noticed the camera? Had the camera simply found his face?

Tavistock remembered how in the next video, Vel moved better when people weren't watching. He was still wearing only a filthy loin cloth and a fur with patches of hair fallen out.

Torch on the graph.

"I was feeling better. One of the sisters had found a cache of jerky and was making sure I ate."

"Did you put the cache of jerky there?" Tavistock asked.

"Started to leave caches after the first video. Some stuff is floating back, more emotional tone than memories of scenes. I wouldn't have been feeling better enough to jump, and I probably was covered with lice, fleas, crabs. Exo-parasites love me. You're going to have to clean me up. Give me miticide shampoo. I've had people give me that shampoo very early on. I remember the smell." Vel turned a bit in the chest strap. "I survived this. I have to remind myself that I did survive this."

The video ended. The examiner turned the lights back up. He looked through the long chart, but didn't say anything. Tavistock keyed Vel's device off again and handed it to him. Vel said, "For the memory hoard?"

Tavistock nodded. The examiner unhooked Vel, put the apparatus in order, and left the room. Vel tucked his shirt back in and put his jacket back on. They didn't see the examiner again. Dora came in and suggested that they go for a little walk before joining the team before dinner. "So glad to finally meet you. I've already met Quince."

"Glad to meet you, too," Vel said. "And you've met Carolyn."

Tavistock said, "We had to know. I believed it, but..."

"It's okay. Don't talk about it right now." Vel's eyes defocused on the present. He laughed. "I see that you mostly won't."

Dora said, "You're checking the futures? If you can see the possibilities, how did you get shot?"

"We can fake each other out. He saw me shot, probably, and didn't see himself dead. I knew there was a chance I'd die, but saw him with a bullet hole in his skull. Saw the hospital restroom, the rest, you know."

Dora said, "We only have your side of the story."

"You don't even have a corpse. Your examiner didn't even ask me about killing Zeus."

Tavistock said, "Not our jurisdiction."

They walked down to the Thames running toward London. Vel looked at it and said, "It used to run across the mammoth plains. We'd follow it into what became Germany. Always good water, full of fish."

Dora said, "Bet it wasn't called the Thames, then."

"Something like. It's not so clean now, not as dirty as it was a hundred years ago. No London back 12,000 years ago."

Tavistock said, "Do you ever miss that life?"

Vel said, "I like being clean and free from vermin. And I love clean clothes. I miss some of the people. But they weren't all alive at the same time. When do we need to get back for supper?"

"We can head back now."

Vel's eyes did their future-scan gaze that Tavistock could spot now. Vel said, "We've got a bit more time. Cooper is joining us, but he's about ten minutes away."

Tavistock said, "Some people have speculated that you imitate the people around you. Another person said that if you were a chameleon, you would have been straighter."

"If I do, it's not deliberate. If I'm a natural chameleon, that's naturally what I am." Vel paused, before saying, "Funny that he asked me if I was from space, but didn't ask about the chameleon thing. You must have put that in a report."

Tavistock said, "I did."

Dora said, "Your DNA is missing some of the modern mutations, but you're certainly not alien."

"I'm so glad there was no DNA screening in the eighteenth century. I was arrested then for being in a Molly House."

Tavistock's mobile rang as Vel was speaking. Tavistock answered and heard that the team had supper ready at the safe house. Peter Cooper was joining Dora, Tavistock, and Vel. Vel wasn't to see the rest of the team, just in case.

They walked back a shorter way than they'd come. The team had brought in catered food: roast beef, a Yorkshire pudding that was still hot, turnips, sprouts, and a Stilton cheese—pure British cooking. Cooper grinned at them.

"What, no Spotted Dick?" Vel said, understanding what they were presenting here.

Cooper said, "We have got custard for after." They were all British here, even Vel after his own country died to become the English Channel.

The sprouts, not cooked soggy, had un-British hints of nutmeg. The beef was superb. No one talked about the lie detector test or the video or the device that Vel now had in his pocket. Cooper said, "I'm delighted to finally meet you. Quince has told me so much about you."

Vel paused with a fork of beef in his hand and said, "I'm glad we're working together."

Cooper said, "Took a bit. We didn't know what to believe."

After the boiled custard, they sat around with port, biscuits, and the Stilton. Vel leaned back away from the port and cheese, and said, "I want to have my passport back, so I can return to Emil."

"Shouldn't you be here to help?" Cooper asked.

"I don't want to see my double. I'll need to go to the campsite when he's in now time and clean up the twenty-first-century meat wrappers. Set up cameras so I can find out what happened." He paused, looked at the port, perhaps, Tavistock thought, remembering his Solstice hangover. "I can feel doubles, a sort of telepathy. Don't want to be too close to him. He'll be coming forward in time to sleep safely for maybe a month, and I'll be dealing with the cameras and the food wrappers."

"Quince already told us he'd ask for this," Dora said. "Why not?"

Cooper said, "The Powers that Be request that you plead guilty to passport violations and pay a fine. If you don't have your bank card with you, we can get your bank to send over a cashier's check. We've put a hold for the amount on your bank account. We'll give you back a passport identical to the one you had. In the future, we'll take care of your passports, unless you're naturalized there."

"If I jump to the contemporary UK, should I call in advance?"

"Time travel? Yes, that would be a good idea. Can't you afford to fly normally?"

"Jumping's way cheaper. And I didn't have an exit visa for the last trip I did by jumping, so I'll have to jump back. I don't know what your fine's going to be yet. I do have a bank card in my wallet."

"We'll have a card reader with the judge."

"How soon?" Tavistock asked. "Do you have a judge on tap? Courtroom?"

Cooper said, "We've got a judge who's authorized to make house calls if it's a matter of national security. He's on his way with a bailiff and court reporter."

Vel asked, "Has he read all the reports on me? And Diana and Quince?

Cooper said, "We've given him as complete a report as possible, and he'll have today's results, too."

Vel said, "He'll be more comfortable if I wear the anklet when I go in to see him." He pulled the anklet out of his pocket and handed it back to Tavistock, then put his foot up on one of the chairs.

The judge, his bailiff, and the court recorder showed up at 9 p.m. Vel went in alone to talk to them. Cooper handed Tavistock Vel's new government-approved passport, then said, "Marcus will go with him to help with the cameras. Marcus doesn't like foreign assignments, but we got Marcus to take the assignment anyway because of the shiny machines to play with. So Vel settled a house on the family for his boy?"

Tavistock said, "Man, not a boy. Apparently not intimidated by any of this. A doctor who works from time to time for Médecins Sans Frontières."

Marcus came in while Vel was still with the judge. "He's very cute for a caveman.

Dora said, "The doctor's quite presentable, too."

"Interesting technical problem with the cameras. I can do better than he did with the first videos."

"Bring your partner. Otherwise, you'll be watching them a bit too much," Cooper said.

"No partner right now. Could I get Vel to loan me one of the family boys?"

Tavistock said, "He left all the gay kin in England. They're very pissed."

"I saw the surveillance videos. They're quite nice looking when they're cross. Black-headed girl is Vel's daughter, right?"

Dora said, "It's dyed, though that might be close to her real hair color."

Marcus said, "I'll try to get sound with the next camera traps. And some zooms. Be interesting to see if anyone can crack the language."

Tavistock wished he was the one going to Bratislava with the toys, but Vel told him he was the one who helped him in England, a much messier role.

Dora said, "Nobody, including him, is likely to know the language more than 12,000 years afterward."

Cooper said, "If someone was yelling, that would have an obvious meaning."

Tavistock thought that technical problems seduced Marcus more than other humans.

Then Vel came back and sat on a couch with his legs up, bent, arms wrapped around his legs. Cooper said, "Shouldn't sit like that in a good suit. Kinda showing off with the buttons, weren't you? You can take the suit off without unbuttoning the sleeves."

Vel said, "It will have to be cleaned anyway." He paused, not looking at anyone. "I was scolded."

Tavistock asked, "Is it done?"

"Not quite yet. I'm supposed to feel anxious and guilty for a while. Me, guilty? When taking me apart while I was under general anesthesia was an option."

Cooper said, "I'm glad we didn't."

Vel said, "How could that man make me feel guilty?" He finally noticed Marcus.

Cooper said, "Sorry, I didn't introduce you. Marcus will be helping you with the cameras. He's our best technical boy."

Marcus said, "He's a judge. They're good at making people feel guilty."

Vel sat wrapped tight until the bailiff, with a copy of the official judgment in his hand, called Vel back in. Tavistock handed him his new passport with the government-approved lies about his birthday. Vel, ignoring the bailiff's motioning hand for a moment, said, "You'll find the double after New Years. Quince will know more precisely. Most of the times when people took me home, they fucked me or I gave them blow jobs, but I'd had some people take me home and just clean me up and feed me and try to get me help, even hide me from Immigration. So, I'd...he...the double won't be surprised whatever you do. He'll also be used to cars. Also, don't be surprised if I know a little rent-boy English. Like, "blow job pizza.""

Vel disappeared into the judge's makeshift chambers, then came out with the paperwork signed. He said, "I used to time-jump up-time more before I realized what it was. I thought I was simply traveling to other places on the planet, magic lands. By the way, that was a nasty fine."

As Tavistock took the anklet off for the last time and handed it to Vel, he said, "From now on, you know what happens, right?"

"All over except the emotions," Vel said. "Marcus, see you in Bratislava. Tavistock, Cooper, I'll have my number transferred to a new mobile. My email account is Channel.Lands@gmail.com.

Vel stepped across England, the Channel, France, Germany, and the rest into the time of the apartment he shared with Emil. Marcus flew east the more mundane way, with boxes full of his toys. Emil and his family greeted Vel warmly and found a hotel room for Marcus in the efficient way of an old European family dealing with a potential mistress. Vel suggested that Tavistock's team clear some of the young gay men in his family and bring them over for Marcus to choose from. This made the kids who'd felt left out happy enough, and Marcus reported that they were good company. They all found the Bratislava club and seemed to adjust to local customs quite well.

Vel hired a brother-in-law to manage the mammoth farm's tourist business. One of his straight nephews had already married another of his in-laws. The old man took Vel hunting. They got a boar, which served as the centerpiece of a late Slavic Christmas.

Vel and Emil were asleep, full of roast boar and ice wine and probably each other, when Quince called Tavistock. "Young Vel is in town by a Soho club. He'll need a warm jacket. I can't join you—time-trap—but I'll direct you by mobile. Get a cab. Carolyn will call you after you've got him."

Tavistock met Simon at the club. An older man had the young Vel braced against the wall, and was babbling at him, his hand dabbing at Vel's jeans. The younger Vel wore a filthy pair of jeans—either carried with him through the late Paleolithic assault or which he'd just found in a skip. Simon stood about ten feet away while Tavistock went in closer and said, "Buzz off."

The older man said, "He's my partner, just a bit drunk."

"No, really fuck off," Tavistock said, pulling his warrant card. "We know he's not your partner." The man let Vel slide down the wall. Tavistock sent Simon across the street for miso soup with extra bean curd. He gave Vel the hoodie, which the boy knew how to pull on.

They had to hold the young Vel up to get him to a table. The present-day Vel had told Tavistock that a long jump could take as much as a thousand calories. Simon fixed young Vel a tea with lots of sugar. Quince said on the mobile, "I can feel him. I'm ringing off. Call Dad."

Tavistock called Bratislava, feeling time distort around him. They got the soup and sweet tea down this Vel, who started to say something. Tavistock really didn't want it to be "blow job?" The boy-Vel's eyes did the defocused look at his possibilities in this strange place. The Sight appeared to be difficult, but maybe he only looked into a few minutes ahead, enough to know not to ask if he should blow the two men feeding him tea and soup. He pulled back into the present and looked back at the counter with the sushi, back at Tavistock and Simon, then back at the slices of tuna, like a dog telling an owner he wanted cheese out of the refrigerator. Tavistock bought basic slices of raw fish, no rice. Vel ate it delicately with his fingers, without dipping it into the sauces. He had to pause when he shivered too much.

His single braid going down his bare back had looked as filthy as his jeans. Tavistock wondered if he'd mind if they cut off the braid and gave him a contemporary haircut.

Carolyn called Tavistock. "Get him to yours, put him in a hot shower, feed him as much as he wants. At that point in history, people are used to almost starving, then gorging. But make it raw meat, protein that has Vitamin C, not cooked meat. I'll meet you at your house. Quince is time-locked out. Pity. We could explain things to him through her. Vel Prime is feeling the desperation and fear all the way across Europe."

Vel Double and Tavistock got into the cab after Tavistock paid the cabby extra for letting the boy into the cab. Simon didn't get in; he had other things to do the rest of the night.

Isobel and Patrick had gone away when he said he needed privacy for business. She'd told him she had an aunt in Yorkshire. Tavistock had insecticidal shampoo waiting in the shower, along with a drench for crabs that he'd let Carolyn apply.

This Vel paused at the door. He sniffed—smelling woman perhaps, or a cousin, then came in, not sitting on anything, and gave a quick glance at the grand piano. Tavistock showed him to the shower, turned on the water, adjusted it to comfortably warm, and handed him the bottle. Vel, still shivering, bobbed his head, knowing what to do with it. While the boy Vel was in the shower, Tavistock put the jeans and the hoodie in double plastic bags for incineration. He laid out fresh jeans, a pair of briefs, and a linen nightshirt.

The boy had even found the crab drench and used that too, Tavistock discovered when Vel came out wrapped in a towel. Wobbling on his feet, a hand against the wall, Vel pulled on both the jeans and the nightshirt. Carolyn arrived about then, so Tavistock let her in and introduced her to Vel, hoping the doubled forward Vel would at least get the intent. While Carolyn checked Vel's temperature, Tavistock went in to spray the bathroom. When Tavistock came back, Carolyn said, "There's blood on the towels. If he had a clue as to what we were doing, I'd like to hospitalize him, but given that if we drug him and he wakes up with a greasy butt, what do you think he'll think happened? If it comes through the jeans, feed him a low-residue diet for now. He needs to trust us and to stay put until he recovers a bit. The arrow wound has closed. Your surgeons will pull that out in about 12,000 years, his time." She handed Tavistock a bag. "Some re-hydration fluid if there's any diarrhea. He's borderline hypothermic. Let's see about warmed blankets. Do you have a clothes dryer?"

Tavistock called Vel Prime to see if he had more suggestions. He didn't. Vel Double seemed nonplussed to see Tavistock talking into a small plastic object. Magic here was different. Carolyn watched him and said, "I hope he's housebroken. I can show myself out. I'm leaving a bowl of mint cakes on your piano. For when he starts jumping again."

After Carolyn left, Tavistock lead Vel Double to the bed set up in Patrick's room. The boy got into it, turned belly up and stared at Tavistock, watched him walk to the door and turn off the lights. They'd set up an infrared camera trained on the bed. Tavistock left the door cracked slightly, remembering Vel Prime's need of company, at least nearby, at night. After Tavistock was out of the hall, in his own bedroom, Vel Double got up and opened the door all the way, then stood in the doorway a moment before going back to bed. He began weeping quietly, leaking tears as he'd done after he'd woken up from the surgery.

Tavistock heated a blanket in Isobel's clothes dryer and took it in to wrap around Vel, who turned to tuck the warmth in around him.

Tavistock called Vel again. "He's crying."

"You have a camera on him. Keep him away from knives."

"He's just quietly crying."

"I can feel him. He's lost everything that matters to him. I doubt he has a plan yet. You can't do anything except make sure he doesn't decide to—"

"I can't just let him cry."

"He going to get enough to eat and he's warming up. He's not lousy now, and he's not getting raped. I told you it would be emotional. Clean jeans and clean shirts, full belly, warm bed—he'll start feeling better. Then he'll start thinking."

"I want to get him a haircut. That braid is probably still lousy."

"Better do that tomorrow before he tries trading someone a blow job for a haircut. I always liked to match my time."

"I feel like he should be in hospital."

"No."

"Is it late there?"

"No, I'm just being a bit cold to keep from being overwhelmed by his pain myself. Call me at any time. If we're in the middle of something, I'll call you back."

Tavistock heard Emil whispering behind Vel, his body moving on the bed. Vel said, "He survives this. I'm here. You're with him."

Tavistock said, "He looks so young."

"Two thousand years old. This is a puberty cycle, maybe triggered by bad conditions. I don't think I realized my New Orleans was in the future until later than his time. Call me when he wakes up. Quince says he'll start making you breakfast day after tomorrow."

"Carolyn said she hopes he's housebroken."

"He's seen and used modern toilets before. I figured those out in New Orleans second time I was there."

In the morning, Tavistock asked Simon to come help wash Vel Double's hair over the kitchen sink. After they'd finished washing the hair (Vel didn't squirm too much), they sat Vel on a kitchen chair, front to back, and combed out the long wavy hair. Vel held his back and shoulders rigid, but relaxed his neck slightly, seeming to take pleasure in the touch. The heat of the dryer, and the comb

and brush in his hair were social grooming. Simon knew
from Scouting how to do braids. Tavistock stepped back
to crowd the boy less, and saw Vel's back slump slightly.
He started cooking fried eggs and bacon rashers, and Vel
twisted in the chair to watch him. Vel's hands echoed the
movements of Tavistock's hands. The toaster's pop-up
mechanism seemed to startle him.

Simon said, "We've got a laptop checked out that he
can use if he can figure it out. Cooper and someone else
have a bet on his being able to learn how to play Solitaire.
It will keep him occupied."

"I'm working from home, so I can help him. Does his
machine have net access?"

"That would be pushing things."

The first day Tavistock worked from home, he
showed Vel how a mouse worked and tried to get him to
recognize the pattern of the game. The boy simply moved
cards around for most of the morning between trips to
the refrigerator for chunks of the various meats, including a fresh lamb stomach with greens that the Somerset
folks sent, though Tavistock doubted that was low residue
exactly.

After a more formal lunch at the dining room table,
Vel, muttering in a dead language, walked around touching furniture while Tavistock cleaned up after lunch.
Then the younger Vel sat back down to the computer and
looked at each card very carefully. Tavistock leaned over
his shoulder, took the mouse gently from his fingers, and
moved an ace, then a two and three, then did a bit of fill-
ing in under a King. He gave Vel the mouse again. Vel
cautiously moved another ace. Tavistock showed him how
to display other cards. Vel worked slowly, seeing what the

machine would and wouldn't let him do. He could apparently count the numbers of diamonds, spades, hearts, and clubs, even if he couldn't recognize the numeric figures. Tavistock had learned that people began counting and using tally marks farther back in the Paleolithic than what he thought he'd been taught as a child. The boy was holding up under all this rather well, Tavistock thought.

Vel muttered at the computer after an hour of not getting a score. He looked hard at Tavistock, then at the door. Time to go out. Vel Prime said to take Vel Double to a camping supply store and buy him a backpack no more than nine inches deep, which he could use to move produce when time-jumping. Young Vel seemed curious about the packs, but more curious about the hair cutters. Tavistock bought him a broad and long but shallow pack with cincher straps.

Next, Vel led Tavistock into a unisex hair place. Smiling, Vel watched as the stylists moved around the customers. Tavistock found a stylist who was free. Vel found a free chair and sat down. Tavistock explained to the stylist that the boy was foreign and didn't know British customs. The stylist pulled the braid apart and sighed. He cut off Vel's hair at chin length before styling it. Vel watched in the mirror, turning his head under pressure from the stylist's fingers.

"Mute?" the stylist said. "Cute."

"Doesn't speak English," Tavistock said. He guessed the word, *blowjob*, floated around the next second's possibilities.

The next morning, as predicted, Tavistock woke to toast, eggs, and rashers of bacon. Vel grinned from the other side of the table. Vel's older self phoned and said, "He's feeling physically better."

"He seems more physically resilient than you."

"He just had some anal fissures and a tiny arrowhead to the hip. I was gutted like a deer to repair gunshot to the bowel and two major blood vessels. And my bruised kidney was treated conservatively, as in allowed to heal on its own."

"He was starving."

"Yes, he was starving." Vel's tone pushed Tavistock away from any further attempts to tease. Vel said, "He hasn't been back yet. When he does go back, only a few hours might have passed in his time, that past. Or months. But I can't go back until he does, apparently. He could spend years here, then go back, with a beard and all his body hair back."

"I can't take care of him for years."

"I'll let you know when I can get back to set new camera traps. We'll have sound. You let me know when he disappears for a few hours with the pack. I'm sure you've got him under 24/7 surveillance."

"He's learning how to play Solitaire."

Vel laughed, and explained to Emil, whose laugh rumbled through Vel's chest. "I've felt like I've known how to play Solitaire since forever. Now I know when I learned it."

"Doesn't that corrupt the past or something?"

"The past is already corrupt. Call me when you need me." *And not all the time* was the subtext.

Vel Double had been playing Solitaire as Tavistock talked to Vel Prime. The boy didn't quite look like a contemporary, but Tavistock couldn't figure out precisely why not. The imitation was improving, as was his game.

The next day, Tavistock gave Vel Double a key and showed him how to use it. He began taking longer and longer walks under surveillance. A week passed before Tavistock found his refrigerator full of food he hadn't bought: eggs, oranges, two loaves of pumpernickel, and a ham. As Tavistock was looking into his refrigerator, Vel Prime called. "Check your email. I was able to go back last night. We got something quite interesting on the camera traps."

Vel Double walked in with his pack bulging, pulled out a steak, and tried to hand it to Tavistock, realized Tavistock had his hands full, laid the steak on the table and stepped out of sight through time, with a sideways glance back at Tavistock.

"He's just gone back," Tavistock said. "Again."

"We're sending a surveillance tape from a grocery store near you. Marcus just got it from CCTV."

At the grocery store meat counter, Vel left no time between frames, but his pack went from empty to full and then recycled a few times.

Now looking quite exhausted, Vel stepped to Tavistock's present, the backpack flaccid against his back. He smiled at Tavistock and went to the basket of Kendal Mint Cakes on the grand piano, took one, then walked to the kitchen. Tavistock heard the water running into a glass. Tavistock put Vel Prime's video on the file server for the rest of the team before he watched it himself.

Vel had returned to the Younger Dryas with food and more hostility than Tavistock had seen in the earlier videos. In spurts of seconds, the boy time-jumped around, waving an anachronistic steel blade. The man who'd tried to control him by hurting him shot an arrow at him again, but Vel, not near starving this time, shifted in time and grabbed the arrow with his off hand, still holding the knife in his right.

Behind Tavistock, the young Vel, crunching mint cake and drinking water, watched the video, too. The headman began a tirade. The Vel in the video stopped and stared at the man, then said something that started off another tirade. The man who'd hurt and raped Vel sank to his knees. Vel didn't turn his back on the headman but sidled up to his torturer. Behind Tavistock, Vel stopped breaking off pieces of mint cake with his teeth and grunted slightly, seeing himself on the video. The boy put his steel knife to his torturer's throat.

The headman said something emotionless. Tavistock guessed, "Go ahead. Kill him."

Vel put his hand on Tavistock's shoulder. Tavistock tried not to flinch. In the video, Vel looked at one of the women, said something soft and pained in what seemed like another language.

The woman had said whatever older sisters or nieces say, probably about the stupidity of blood feud. Vel pulled the blade away from the torturer's throat, but couldn't resist kicking him to the ground. They stared at each other, and Tavistock felt the deeper breathing of the boy behind him, leaning into his shoulders to see the video better. The torturer stared up from the dirt, said something hostile and taunting. In the video, Vel replied with scornful words, which he repeated to Tavistock as though he'd understand them, then again, shorter, with a different sound at the end of the phrase. Tavistock guessed this was "I can sleep somewhere else." "I can sleep here." Vel on screen pulled a chunk of ham out of his pack and cut a piece for the headman.

Vel Prime had put a voice-over at the end of the video. "I think that the exchange after Vel kicked the rapist was 'You have to sleep some time and your women can't protect you,' and the reply was, 'I can sleep elsewhere.'"

Marcus's voice note was "I'd have killed the guy, but I'm glad he didn't."

The next video was in a new location. Vel had forced them to start moving by not bringing the food back to the camp, but caching it a bit further south.

The distances would get longer as they got stronger.

Vel's cover email also explained the micro-jumps in the surveillance video from the store—the stores had CCTV cameras, and Vel Double could see that if they could see him steal, bad things could happen.

Tavistock turned to look at the younger Vel and nodded, hoping that he would take it as assurance that he could sleep here. The boy padded away in his bare feet and ate some meat he'd stashed in the refrigerator earlier, then went to the room where he'd been sleeping. Tavistock and Simon began researching ways to trap time-jumping shoplifters. Vel Prime might pay for these damages, but not all of his cousins could be trusted to care what the dying ones might think about having their property stolen.

Back in time, a small young girl about two was cold and stiff two mornings later. Her mother, dry eyed, knelt, rocking slightly, by the tiny body. Despite the new food and the bladders of re-hydration fluid, she'd died. Her mother smoothed out her limbs, not sure they'd let the girl's body go to the dark rather than eating her. Vel began building a pyre and stared down the men, who allowed him to burn the body. He sat by the embers for over an hour before walking off into the dark.

Vel Double came back to the house and didn't look at Tavistock, just went into his room, avoiding the nightly review of the videos. Marcus reported that Vel Prime was also very quiet, not talking about the death.

Then the operation went into overdrive. Younger Vel stole food and cached it. Older Vel set the cameras around the caches and guarded them, eating and sleeping when it was daylight for the band. Vel Prime said, "I think you need to let your wife come home. Let's shift him to the Somerset house. We can set up caches for him to steal at wholesale cost for the meat."

Tavistock said, "Sorry about the little girl."

"If they'd stayed put, they all would have died."

Tavistock and Simon coaxed Vel the Younger into a car and drove him to Somerset. By now, he trusted them, but he began to fidget after a half hour in the car. They stopped by the Thames near where Tavistock had walked with Vel Prime. The young Vel looked at the river and back at Tavistock and Simon, and then pivoted to see the landscape under the buildings. Tavistock realized that if Vel did recognize the river in its new beds, he might wonder why the river he knew ran through strange pierced buildings, bubbles of glass and masonry, and frozen gravel streets.

Vel got back into the car. They drove on to Somerset and took him inside the house. The men who had taken care of Vel Prime earlier, when he was recovering from the gunshot, watched him. He was still skinnier than Vel Prime, but had the beginning of a beard coming in that he shaved with Tavistock's razor that morning. Vel said something in a language that had died without modern issue.

Simon brought in Vel's laptop with the card games on it.

One of the men said, "What does he know? What's he doing?"

Tavistock said, "He's provisioning about fifteen people. A very young girl died. I don't know what he knows, but I get the impression he's picking up some English. We're going to set up caches he'll think he's stealing. Just keep a lot of Kendal Mint Cakes handy. And orange juice and diluted sports drinks. Time jumping seems to be fueled on glucose."

Simon said, "We showed him the Thames. He looked around, but didn't seem excited. Didn't show any sign of real recognition."

"So, we're another set of magicians," the other man said.

Tavistock and the two *soi-disant* nephews walked Vel by people moving meat from a truck to a trailer about a half-mile from the house. Tavistock and the two men who lived in the house pretended not to notice the Young Vel's interest in the meat trailer.

He nailed it a half hour later. Tavistock found him asleep on the bed in the kitchen, his shirt covered with meat juices, rather alarming at first until Vel Senior sent the night's videos.

Tavistock went back to his wife and son and tried to do other things and rebuild her trust. She said, when she walked in the door, "You brought work home." Tavistock wondered what the cousins knew about Vel. The neighbors apparently thought he'd had an affair with the boy, but she never mentioned that, just was cold and distant.

Tavistock let it go. She was back in his bed. She gave him a spectacular blowjob, leaving him limp and dazed, then sat watching him with clinical eyes, as if seeing how addicted he was to her. Tavistock was both anxious and aroused by the distance combined with the technique. La Belle Dame Sans Merci—he padded out of bed naked to find the Keats when he thought she was asleep. She followed him to the book and said, "Oh, Keats, what a fussy little boy."

"The woman had her regrets, apparently."

"The woman always has her regrets," Isobel said as she turned him back toward the bed. Tavistock wondered what the people monitoring him would make of this, but apparently, either it wasn't his night to be monitored—a courtesy for the time he'd been without his wife—or they didn't ride the allusions all the way down. Tavistock even wondered if he was just fantasizing about his own perfectly mortal wife being one of the long-lived creatures. Vel would move on out of his life, and he'd be back to chasing more mundane border jumpers. He'd die and Vel and Quince and Diana would keep living. *I've run off with the fairies.*

The young Vel moved the band through the territory of another band, where there was not enough game for both bands, and knew that the game would disappear as the cold sank further south. He bribed his way though with meat that doubled Vel Prime's meat bill for the next few days. The big fear was that this second band would follow them and steal the caches. Vel Prime went back with a flaming sword and fluorescent garments and a wig that glowed and swirled in the dark, and put the fear into them. Vel Prime's comment on the tape was "Assholes."

The band began to find game, mostly nearly fat-free snow hares. They ran into a third band, which spoke a language the troop leader knew. One night, the headman took away the man who'd raped Vel and came back with a blond boy who looked like he was fourteen, but whose eyes seemed older. He pushed the boy toward Vel, a peace offering. Vel, who shared a language with the boy, seemed to have reservations about the whole thing.

The younger Vel still slept in the Somerset House, a month and a half into this. The band was walking to France. Vel Prime seemed to shut down sexually as much as Vel Double, Marcus said in a report to the group. Emil wasn't pressuring him, but asked if he could visit the younger Vel. Vel said yes, and Emil arranged a duty swap with another Médecins Sans Frontières doctor in Bath.

Emil went to the house for dinner on his first free night. He kissed Vel Double on the lips the third time he came to dinner, just before he walked out the door, not looking back to see the young Vel's reaction. At first, the boy cringed, sure nothing good was coming of this. One night he stayed with the band rather than come up-time to Somerset. But Tavistock's team served up the steal-able meat, and game was still scarce. Young Vel came back. Emil stayed away that night. The next two times he came to dinner, he didn't go near young Vel at all. Time after that, Emil planted a chaste kiss on Vel's nose.

This went on for nearly a month while the band crossed plains that used to be full of mammoths, almost to France. Tavistock wondered if Vel was taking the band to the cave region.

Vel Prime finally remembered Emil from 12,000 years ago, or said he did. The people at the house said that young Vel was learning English as fast as he could, wanted to learn what to say to get people not to go, to stay.

Vel's kinsmen taught him.

Emil came to dinner. The cousins gave Vel a small glass of wine, not more. Young Vel drank the wine as though he knew its effects. He motioned for more, but they refused to give him more. Emil wasn't going to cheat on this one. He finished his dinner, then walked to Vel's chair. Vel was still seated at the table, flushed and quivering slightly, sweat on his neck and face.

With just his fingertips, Emil turned Vel's head and kissed him full on the lips, lingering a bit, then straightened up and started for the kitchen door.

"No. Don't go. Stay," Vel said in English. He stood up.

Emil came back and knelt in front of Vel. He kissed the zipper over Vel's cock, still not pushing. "Unless you have an erection for me, I don't go further." The boy got the intonation if not any of the words and grabbed Emil's head and held it against his crotch. After a moment, Emil slowly moved Vel's hands away and led Vel upstairs to the big bed.

Afterward, Emil called Vel Prime to say, "He had a hard-on for me. I blew him. That bastard hadn't hurt his cock. I was afraid to go anywhere else."

Vel Prime said, "Stay with him tonight. I'm not jealous."

Emil said, "And they're not intercepting this call."

"Okay, I'm a little bit jealous."

Within two days, the young Vel had gone back to his own time and tried Emil's tactics on the young boy the headman had given him.

The young boy put up with two nights of chaste kisses. On the third night, he tapped Vel Double on the shoulder. Vel Prime and Marcus cut the video after the blonde's big aggressive kiss. Marcus and Vel said in the voice-over that they knew straight guys could find queer sex scenes squirm-inducing. The video skipped to the headman coming up while Vel was asleep in the boy's arms. Teeth bared, the little blond stared back at the leader, ready to kill for Vel now. The headman smiled and backed off. Vel's oldest niece, looking slightly pregnant, opened her sleeping furs for the headman. He kissed her and said something. Vel's voice-over was, "They finally made their young god happy."

Emil met Tavistock at Gatwick for drinks before he flew back home. Emil said, "Thrown over for a teenaged blond."

"You still have Vel Prime."

"He says he's going to go through adolescence before I die. Now I know what I have to look forward to. I love Vel, any age."

"You think Vel really remembered you from 12,000 years ago? He said he didn't remember any of this before."

"Random floating memory perhaps, not connected to any particular time. Or he lied to make me happy. I don't care which."

Vel met Emil at the airport, and in a few days Marcus said that Vel and Emil seemed quite a bit more cheerful. Marcus and Vel had designed better and better surveillance cameras, including one that had an array of small lenses that would look like mica or quartz grain glitter on a rock but that could put together a large detailed video they could crop from. Vel continued to work on the late Paleolithic clothes for his younger self. Marcus seemed happy enough with one of Vel's nephews.

Cooper called a meeting in the usual place, with Marcus on speakerphone from the British embassy in Bratislava. Cooper said, "We think it's time to cut the boy off from the up-time supply line. Quince said she could get out of the time-lock in about two days. She'll try to explain what's been happening to him, and more important-ly, what will happen. We've got the device that will catch him. We've got a drug to sedate him while we change him into the clothes Vel Prime made for him. And we're going to shoot him with something colorful in the way of paint balls so his people know not to try to talk him into return-ing. We could do all this without trying to explain to him, but Carolyn and Quince persuaded us that it would only be fair to try to tell him what was going to happen. We want him to understand that he isn't to come back here to steal."

Tavistock stared at the table, not wanting to look at Cooper. He intellectually understood the reason for the physical demonstration, but the boy had been through so much.

Cooper had Tavistock and Simon come with him and Quince to the Somerset house. Vel watched them come in, jittering in and out of their present. Cooper had Si-mon turn on a machine, and Vel stopped moving. Quince touched him. He stiffened, walked over to the bed in the kitchen and squatted on it, to be at their height sitting. Quince sat on the floor beside the bed. She didn't touch him again right away. They stared at each other, at the possible futures they could dive into. Pick one.

He gave her his hand, jerked it back.

Quince said, "It's confusion in there. He knows you can trap him now."

Marcus and Vel Prime had perfected that technology, Vel's pay-back for 150 years of bad passports. Tavistock wished he'd been the technical boy for the project rather than Vel Double's keeper.

Tavistock asked, "Does he know he's in the future?"

Quince shook her head. "He doesn't believe he could possibly be my father since he doesn't fuck women. We're stronger gods than he is, bigger liars. I didn't tell him that he will fuck women in the future, and I'm also a descendent of the children he sired. Family has collected his genetic material. Line breeding, a bit icky to think about."

The men sat down on the kitchen chairs, giving Quince and Vel some space.

Tavistock asked, "Can we tell him what we need to do? Will it make it easier?"

Quince said, "He knows. He needs an excuse to stop coming here." She reached for the young Vel's hand again. "He wants to stay. The gods are kind in this house. But he knows he can't."

"If you'd have explained things earlier —"

She again touched the boy who'd become her father. "He'd lost all hope. He'd have just given up. He had to find his own plan to survive. Lost in the magic place." She released his hand. "He doesn't know if this is a future time or not. Doesn't really care. It's some other place for him. He wants the people he loved to stop aging and dying."

"Can't do a damned thing about that, yet," Tavistock said.

Quince said, "He'll have to learn to accept it. He wants to know your plans. You can speak them, and I'll translate to him."

"Your father suggested this, "Cooper said. "We trap him. Knock him out because we want to change him out of twenty-first-century clothes and give him a bit of a medical check-up, put him in clothes Vel's been making for him, and swat him on the ass with a paintball pellet, frozen slushy so it stings, just when he jumps. Emil's flying in to put him in the deerskin clothes. I think Vel Prime will leave the women a buffalo robe. Don't tell this Vel about Emil, though."

Quince reached for Vel's hand again. His back stiffened, and he nodded at Tavistock.

"He needs an excuse not to come back. For the headman," Quince said. "And he sees that he doesn't come back here. He'd like to stay. Halfway like to stay."

Cooper nodded at Simon who turned off the machine. Vel flicked out of the present. Tavistock wondered if he'd just vanish, go off and find someone else who took in waifs, but Quince was still there, which meant he lived through the 12,000 years between the Younger Dryas and when Carolyn talked him into siring Quince. Quince said, "He's going to look at London before he goes back."

Cooper said, "I wish he'd asked."

The team set up the meat trailer on a bare pasture hill and laid the trap. Vel came, and the trap-field grabbed him. Tavistock watched Vel really struggling against the trap field, almost panicking, maybe wondering if the gods had lied to him. Then he saw Tavistock and stopped struggling. Tavistock couldn't be the one to dart him. Still feeling like a villain, he watched Simon shoot the dart into Vel. The boy slowly sank to the ground.

Emil who'd been hiding out of sight ran in with the Late Paleolithic clothes. He put his mobile on speaker. Vel Prime talked him through how to dress a man in a belt with leggings and a loincloth, how to fit the undertunic and the overtunic. Emil moved Vel's arms and legs. Carolyn joined him to help.

Tavistock remembered the orderlies moving Vel's legs when they prepped him for surgery. Emil put a wolf-tooth necklace around Vel's head, then a string of amber wolf-head beads over that. The amber beads had been Vel's, but one of the band had stolen them when Vel was hurt. Vel Prime had stolen them back. Vel's beads were around his neck again. The gods were kind.

Emil knelt, holding one of Vel's hands until Tavistock urged him to leave before Vel woke up and saw him there. Emil had been Vel's one unadulterated good on this mission. Emil stood up, blinking, and moved behind one of the outbuildings below the hill to be out of sight. Cooper, the best shot of the group, stood waiting with the paintball gun.

When Vel woke up, he felt his wolf beads and stood up slowly, not apparently surprised to find himself in deerskins. He faced Cooper and said, "Soon," began to turn and said, "Do it."

Cooper shot him with the paintball gun, multiple hits. Some of the green spattered the contemporary air. Most of it disappeared with him.

Vel Prime sent the team the video of Vel rolling out of thin air, his left flank and buttock all green. He lay on the ground on his side, quivering, explaining in tumbled words to the headman. The headman looked at the beads and the man who'd stolen them from Vel earlier when he was wounded. The man who'd had the beads earlier shrugged. Vel stumbled to his feet and handed the man who'd had the amber beads the wolf's tooth necklace.

The women looked at the green stain on Vel's deer skin clothes and brought him the buffalo robe. He took off his boots, wrapped up in the robe, took off the leggings and tunics and handed them to the women. He then lay down curled up in the buffalo robe, sleeping for hours while his little blond lover watched over him. The girls tried to rub out the green stains with snow, then gave up and built a small fire and dried the skin clothes very carefully. The blond boy rubbed them as they dried to keep them soft.

In the morning, Vel put on his still-stained clothes before he untangled and braided the headman's hair. Vel's voice-over was that this was an act of allegiance to the headman. They appeared to talk about the little blond, looking at him as they spoke to each other. Marcus imagined the question was "Is he working out for you?" And Vel's response seemed to be "Quite well."

This Vel never came back to the twenty-first century.

Vel Prime sent three more videos. One was of the band hunting game, Vel and the little blond with spears, too. Vel let the boy take a roe deer. The other men took a brace of grouse and found some birds' nests. They ate well that night.

The second video was of the finding of an old mammoth, tusks broken, so rare a thing that the short-lived men had never seen one. Vel said something, the young blond boy looked at him, and the headman seemed to have decided to let the creature go. Point of honor, perhaps. Last of its kind. Vel had gotten them enough meat. The band moved on. The creature stayed behind despite Vel's knowledge of killing and preserving such beasts. Vel had done enough already. A mammoth's worth of meat beyond what he'd given them would be overkill.

In the last video, the younger Vel found the camera, one of the ones with the array of lenses that should have been such good camouflage. He picked up the camera rock, said, "Go," and smashed the thing.

Vel said in the voice note, "good thing he didn't know what a solid state storage device looked like, but I'll leave him alone to his time for now. Maybe check back in a couple of years from a distance."

Tavistock called Vel Prime and asked, "He didn't remember a damn thing about it?"

"I remember 'the Gods have Gods,' but didn't associate it with anything. I had a sense of a magic house in Somerset, a little bit of what Emil did. Some gut feeling, not visual or verbal, about you. I trusted you. I'd thought I'd always known how to play solitaire on a computer, never remembered when I learned."

Tavistock said, "Sending him back was hard."

"All of us have ancestors who survived to at least breeding age, generally ten or fifteen years beyond that to defend the children coming up."

"So you're staying in Slovakia?"

"For now. Once the gates for people with my sorts of passports are up and running, I'll come back. Someone ordered a seventeenth-century media center. I think I've been made by at least one of the clients. Emil and I will live a quiet enough life for a while. One of the family women will bear him some children to make his father happy with heirs."

Tavistock didn't tell Vel that his younger self wanted the short-lived ones to stop aging and dying.

Vel had to leave his former selves behind him, Tavistock thought. He'd seen things through a different paradigm in a dead language, no linguistic breadcrumbs to lead him from future to past. Objects had to be re-wrapped in a new language the way computer files had to be recopied on new media for the stories to stay with the objects.

Vel said, "I will always have the amber wolf-head beads. I made them for an older god. Crazy man. He killed himself to stop the world. It didn't stop for the rest of us."

Tavistock asked, "What makes something memorable?"

"Stories I tell in each changing language, stories I need to teach me things to remember."

Not much desire to remember the story we've just lived through back then. Move on once the cold ended. Move on to stories that made more sense in more languages. Tavistock said, "I think I understand."

Vel said, "Thank you for helping us. I'd have been lost without my family."

Vel wrote the check that covered the meat and part of the operational costs. The Home Office tasked Tavistock's team with finding and giving new passports to the long-lived ones.

Tavistock found one man who'd been living for centuries working in kitchens, who was scrubbing dishes among a bunch of Pakistanis. No sight, no ability to jump, the man seemed bewildered by the fuss and new passport and tissue samples. Not all of the long-lived ones were any brighter than normal or had any talents besides living on and on, outliving all the people they'd grown up with, all their loves. The man asked if he could leave England freely now. When Tavistock said yes, the man said, "I can go to Paris." He'd been saving money for over fifty years for the time when he could leave.

Tavistock said, "Take the ferry. It's more fun than the Chunnel."

One day, as he wondered how he could deal with his wife, if she was one of the long-lived, and what excuse he'd use for taking in a DNA sample this late in the work he'd been doing, Tavistock came come to find a babysitter with his son. The piano was gone. The babysitter looked anxious. She said, "I have a letter for you."

Tavistock opened it:

> You know why I'm leaving. You brought work home and
> it's closing in on us. You have my son. I'm sorry. If you
> try to find me, I'll consider that an act of hostility. Let
> me go. I loved you. Do understand the tense there.
> Anything I left behind is for you to do what you will with
> it. You have a gift for being taken away by the fairies,
> don't you?

The babysitter, who knew he'd been abandoned, cooked a dinner for both Tavistock and Patrick, who wasn't asking questions. Keats knew this feeling, Tavistock thought. He wanted to talk to Vel, but remembered what Carolyn had said about people needing Vel and forgetting his life went at the same pace as theirs, just for longer. Vel wasn't responsible for this.

"You saw her move out?"

"She paid me in cash, like they do, and got the movers to take out the piano and her clothes and things. You've got to accept it and move on. Women leave, they never come back."

"La Belle Dame Sans Merci,"

"I can't say about the mercy or not. But I've seen men take the news before. We specialize in breakup removals and childcare if a child is left behind. I'm good at listening unless the man threatens me."

Tavistock boggled at that. "Enough women leaving that there's a London company that specializes in abandonment removals?"

"Men, too. Don't take sides, really. She said you weren't handy, or I wouldn't be here alone."

"I would never have hurt her. I was curious." Tavistock remembered Diana taunting Vel, and the people who'd gotten out before they could be offered the new deal and the new passports. Did they have Sight to see something bad coming? "I brought work home."

"Some women don't want to be a mistress to the man's work, you know." The babysitter didn't appear to know anything about the complexities of this separation. "I'll be going on. Here's my card if you need a sitter who understands. We can also send someone else if you don't want to be reminded."

Tavistock noticed then that Patrick was crying as he ate his toast and eggs. "We've got each other," he said to his son. "And you have an aunt in Hull, right?"

Patrick said, "Mom lied about the aunt in Hull. We were back at the commune every time. I could go live there."

Tavistock said, "I've lost track of my own family. We could find them."

Patrick said, "Maybe. Maybe you'll leave me, too."

"I won't."

"I can stay home from school for a week and you won't leave me?"

Tavistock nodded. He would work from home; he'd explain what just happened. What they'd do to him for not telling them his suspicions earlier, he didn't know. Or perhaps just tell them she left him, a normal human leaving.

They cried together over being abandoned by their fairy wife and mother.

Months later, Tavistock heard from Quince that a time-jumping person named Diana Younger, PhD, traveling on an American passport, had come in through the check portal at Gatwick about two days after Vel had come through the same portal on a business trip to London. The people operating the portal were nervous about the people who'd come through so close to each other.

As far as Tavistock knew, only about five people in the whole world who seemed to be the sort of long-lived person who could time-jump had accepted their new travel conditions. One was a Chinese man whose ancient glittering eyes didn't appear to be gay. Another was a part-Cherokee woman who applied for asylum in the UK. She said that her kind, the ones who couldn't jump, had been burned in the past for outliving their grandchildren. The third was an African man from the Cameroons who appeared to be descended, in part, from Europeans who'd returned to Africa thousands of years before. He spoke English, French, and Chinese along with some African languages.

And Vel and Diana. He never knew if Isobel could jump in time or not, and she wasn't cooperating with taking a UK passport that could be traced and reissued from generation to generation. Surveillance cameras caught her last somewhere in Wales. Cooper had Tavistock in for an interrogation. Tavistock said that he'd never been sure that his wife was another creature like Vel, and it had seemed paranoid to speculate. Cooper ran the DNA profiles from Isobel's hair. He suspended Tavistock against a pending larger investigation, but people, including Cooper, still told him how the work was going, testing him perhaps.

Tavistock decided he wanted to see Vel, who'd said in his intake that he'd be in his apartment over the London antique shop for a week. Diana didn't say where she'd be, just in London for pleasure.

Monday was the day that the shop was closed, so Tavistock rang the apartment buzzer. His mobile rang. Vel said, "Wait there. I'm coming back with dry cleaning. Won't be a tick." Tavistock stayed where he was until Vel came round the corner holding an eighteenth-century man's suit, bright blue silk knee breeches and jacket and white lace collar wrapped in plastic that flapped in the breeze. His scalp showed through his buzz cut hair. He

Rebecca Ore

wore backed leather clogs, jeans, and a tee-shirt for his mammoth farm. He handed the cleaning to Tavistock while he fished out his keys, unlocked the door, and took the dry cleaning back from Tavistock. Before opening the door, Vel said, "I can't tell you where she went, why she left, but if you just want to come up and see old family videos and hang out with us for a while, fine. If you start taking your frustration out on us, you can leave." He ran his free hand over his head and said, "Been wearing a wig over a shaved head. Picking up a furniture order."

"Okay," Tavistock said, feeling less sure that visiting Vel was a good idea.

Vel kicked his clogs off as soon as he was inside the apartment entrance at ground level and pulled off the plastic from the dry cleaned silk suit. "I'm also washing clothes. Quince has a sprained ankle. Her mom's on a date with your colleague."

"Not my colleague right now. I've been suspended. Quince has a sprained ankle? Wasn't she watching where she was going?"

"She's heard that one already. Sorry about your wife and your job."

"I got scolded."

"That might be a good sign. If they're not going to jail you, scolding seems to make them happy. Fines make them very happy." Vel went up the stairs in his bare feet, holding the cleaned clothes high. Tavistock followed.

Tavistock was rather surprised by the apartment over the store—wide floorboards treated with something that looked like wax, not high gloss, rough white plaster walls with various recent paintings hanging from white painted molding, one a Julian Freud, and all lit by floor lamps and windows on three sides. A giant flat-screen hung on one wall. By the door was a clothes rack, silent valet with a navy blue suit, jacket hanging on top over a shirt, pants folded on a rung below that, and shoes with socks on the bottom shelf. Vel saw Tavistock turn to look at it and said, "I have some clients who can't be put off."

Diana, also dressed in jeans but with a silk blouse, waved from one wing chair covered in what looked like linen. Quince was on a sofa with her left leg bound around the ankle and foot raised on a pillow. Vel laid the dry cleaned silks over a table and sat down in another chair with a little table beside it and pointed to another wing-back chair for Tavistock.

"Why is she here?" Tavistock asked. He didn't sit down.

"She brought back my screw mount Leica. She found out more about the Leitz family. They saved the Jews they had working for them. She's feeling lonely. There aren't many of us. Quince vouched for her, unless she can fool Quince. Perhaps the Americans have been a bit rough, though she can neither confirm nor deny that."

Diana didn't say anything to Tavistock, either.

"Have a seat," Quince said. "Dad's got some videos of when he was really a boy."

"I used to wondered if I remembered things that were really from my past, or if I made things up to fill in the holes," Vel said. He disappeared into the back and came out with another clothes rack for his dry cleaned clothes.

When Vel pulled off the plastic wrap, Tavistock smelled dry cleaning fluid. Vel waved the silks in the air then put them on the clothes rack. Tavistock asked, "Some of both?"

Rebecca Ore

"I remembered some of this, but not all of it." Vel drew the drapes on the windows in front and to the side of the room. He picked up a remote and clicked it. The large screen began playing a scene of three boys and two girls, one a blonde, the other girl flat-chested, all in furs, Vel as a young man—the very first time he was a young man. They stripped naked and slid and slithered on the corpse of a mammoth.

Vel said, "The blonde girl is with the boy who takes over the troop in a few years, the other boy with me is my first lover, and the girl is Flat Nan, who tagged along and manages to get pregnant despite it all, probably with the help of my first lover. I remembered that right."

"Watch what comes next," Quince said. "Dad can never criticize me about my hair again."

The youngsters bound their hair in braids, and chopped those short with a flint knife against a log. Then they took brands from the fire and burnt frizzles into the hair, daring each other to burn their hair shorter and shorter, dousing it in the snow. At the end, they were all laughing at the each other, hair fuzzed up, bodies covered with mammoth blood and fat.

The boys built a frame of branches, and the video jumped to show the two women splitting the mammoth hide while the boys lay around the fire giggling at them.

Diana said, "First blonde on the planet?"

"First that I ever saw," Vel said. "Mother of all the blondes in Europe perhaps."

Quince said, "It's recessive."

Vel said, "I didn't misremember. I just didn't remember everything. Not the hair."

Quince said, "I suspect you didn't want to give the younger generations ideas."

Diana said, "Tavistock's all nostalgic, aren't you, Tavistock?"

"Whole thing's like I ran off with the fairies." He caught himself before he started talking about his fairy wife, how much he missed her.

Quince said, "It's not *as if* you ran off with the fairies. You *really* ran off with the fairies. Queer fairies at that. Well, obviously not your wife. I don't know about Diana here."

"Yeah. I ran off with the fairies. I guess we mortals left our accounts of what it's like. Vel, what's it like for you?"

"Joe, I like you. I don't know if you want to hear what I'd say."

Diana said, "Try."

Vel said, "We need beer with this." He got up and walked through a door in the rear and brought back beer for all of them except Quince. "Quince, I'll make you chamomile tea, if you want."

Tavistock took the bottle, some Belgian beer he hadn't had before, and sipped, wishing it wasn't quite so cold. "If we're all going to just be uncomfortable together, I'll be on my way."

Vel said, "No, you could have been much worse, so I'll try. I see people partially mirrored in their children, grandchildren, the family throwing the same types over the centuries. It's more complex than Carolyn's idea that the family is like a string of identical pearls. You're not all alike, but I see the grandfather's traits transformed in the grandson, the mother's loveliness repeated in her children, wit that is both hereditary and transformed by a different time."

Diana said, "If you believed in reincarnation—"

Vel interrupted her. "—oh, that would be nice and comforting. I'm too much of a realist. Even if it happens, the people don't know who they were. They're not exactly like their ancestors. I'm the only one who can see the themes and variations. Not a huge amount of comfort there, but some."

Tavistock said, "And me?"

Diana said, "You have a son. You'll live on in him as my mother lives on in me."

Vel and Quince looked down, away. Tavistock said, "He's also half whatever you people are, obviously."

"Yes," Diana said. "Half of what his mother is. Does it horrify you?"

Tavistock said, "Where is this going?"

Diana said, "I'd like a child who wouldn't grow up and die on me in the blink of an eye."

"You've been a bitch to Vel, terrified Quince. Why should I give you my son to father a child on you?"

"I think that's to be between your son and me."

Vel said, "Back off, Diana. I wouldn't want to see you be a mother any time soon."

Tavistock said, "I don't want my son to feel like some goddess's pet dog. Thomas left you because—"

Vel said, "Stop before you get tossed out of here. You have no idea what happened there."

Quince said, "So, what happened? Answer me. You're the one urging me to get deeply involved with lovers who vanish in what's an hour to us, not have casual shags with people I don't care about."

Vel said, "Quince, I'm not completely sure. One thing was he thought I flirted with death knowing it wasn't going to get me. Probably more importantly, he learned he could love old men and be loved as an old man. The brothel had an old man who came in for special clients. He could make middle-aged men feel like boys. I paid for Thomas's session with him. On my credit card." Vel drained his beer and said, "Then you came to me in terror for all the times and variations of my future possible deaths. Carolyn was right. Won't matter how long I've lived when I'm finally dead."

Diana said, "I'm surprised you made it to 14,000."

Vel said, "Me, too, some days. Tavistock, something to show you." He went farther than the kitchen this time and came back with a skull in one hand and a staff circled by a metal snake in the other. The skull had a hole in the brow, a bit above the eyes. The bullet was resting in Vel's palm under the skull. "The guy who tried to kill me."

"Apollo?"

"Two snakes, not one, and that would have been Asclepius, not Apollo for one," Quince said.

"Oh, Mercury, God of Thieves," Tavistock said.

Vel tossed him the bullet. "Yeah."

Diana said, "Now Vel will spend a century or two feeling guilty."

"Sorry that he couldn't make the transition. It's huge and scary, and I'm still not sure it's going to work out."

Quince said, "O the moaning. O the wailing. I spend my whole life on the other side of the transition. Hand me the remote." Vel tossed it to her.

What played came several years after the younger Vel returned to the last of the Paleolithic, taken at a distance. The headman in furs and his trusted men met another group of men, with their women behind them. Vel said, "I think they're kin of a headman who took another path south. Part of the extended tribe that can't hunt together during average conditions, but which gets together for celebrations and feasts during the prime times."

Vel, with a couple of years' worth of braid and beard, and his blond lover, now filled out more and almost Vel's height, hung back until the troop leader called Vel forward. He ducked his head slightly down and sideways, smiling a smile Tavistock had seen on the current Vel, the chameleon's smile of satisfaction with fitting in, and came forward to grasp forearms and hands. Tavistock thought that they'd accepted Vel as a trusted adviser. Then he saw a young woman with the other band, and looked back at Diana. Not quite the same.

"Virgin huntress, sterile, didn't make much difference then," Diana said. "She didn't need all the melodrama you needed to save the people she was with. She remembered this. She knew what Vel had done. The headman talked about it that night, his heroic but humble god who had saved them. She told me about Vel. I couldn't believe that Vel had completely forgotten."

"Women giving advice weren't a direct threat to the male leaders," Quince said. "If Vel led the troop and fed it, he was a threat to the leader. That's the other reason for all the song and drang."

Tavistock said, "I don't think the German quite translates as song."

Vel looked at his beer bottle and said, "I don't remember meeting your mother. Her story, not mine. Memory doesn't work the same for everyone. I've got another couple of loads of dirty clothes to deal with. Quince, you want chamomile tea or not?"

"Rather have a cola."

Vel stood up. "I'll bring one back for you."

Tavistock said, "You really were just sitting around watching old videos, picking up dry cleaning, and washing clothes."

Vel said, "Sometimes that's just the thing to do. And if people are being emotional, it's nice to have tasks punctuate the tears."

Diana began crying. Vel looked at her, into the next few minutes, then shrugged and went off to move the wet clothes to the dryer and bring Quince back a soft drink. Tavistock realized that Isobel abandoning Patrick didn't come close to leaving a teenaged girl completely alone in the middle of Eastern Europe during World War II, however powerful the teenaged girl.

Vel brought back the soda and another beer for Diana, who said to him, "I thought you remembered."

Vel said, "I didn't. I had no idea why you appeared to be so angry at me."

Quince popped open her soda as she said, "I could have been legitimately mad at Dad if he'd died when I was thirteen and I'd been exposed to the spooky people all alone. But he's not your mom and he doesn't owe you a damn thing."

Vel handed Diana a box of tissues with the beer. "Quince, you'll be spending summers with me. Let's see what we can do to make things better. Joe, any interest in World of War Craft?"

Diana said, "Don't leave me the only one crying."

Vel said, "Play with us. I can probably find another computer here."

Quince said, "I could loan her mine, but I need it for school work."

Diana said, "No."

Tavistock said, "Me, I'd appreciate a break from the song and drama for a while."

Between loads of laundry, the two men spent the rest of the afternoon lost in the imaginary world coming through Vel's computers, while the women wrote up reports to their agencies, sending them out on their phones.

September 2010—August 2011, Jinotega, Nicaragua

Author Biography

Rebecca Ore was born in Louisville, KY, out of people from Kentucky and Virginia, Irish Catholic and French Protestant turned Southern Baptist on her mother's side and Welsh and Borderer on her father's. She grew up in South Carolina and fell in love with New York City from a distance, moved there in 1968 and lived on the Upper West Side and Lower East Side for seven years. Somehow, she also attended Columbia University School of General Studies while spending most of her energy in the St. Mark's Poetry Project. In 1975, she moved to San Francisco for almost a year, then moved to Virginia, back and forth several places for several years, finished a Masters in English, then moved to rural Virginia for ten years, writing sf novels and living in her grandparent's house after they died. Next came homeownership of a small house in Philadelphia with a walled garden, one wall stone and brick, one wall stone against a hill, and the west wall not there, since the neighbor and she shared the space.

She's been mostly an academic gypsy and has been variously an editorial assistant for the Science Fiction Book Club, a reporter/photographer for the Patrick County *Enterprise*, and a assistant landscape gardener. She left Philadelphia after 12 years and ended up in the Virginia suburbs of Washington, DC, for a time. She is currently retired and living in Nicaragua after working for government sub-contractors for over a year.

also by Rebecca Ore— a collection of Vel's tales

Centuries Ago and Very Fast

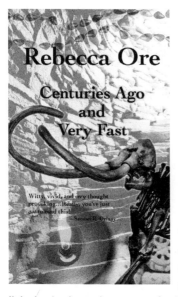

Finalist for the Philip K. Dick and Lambda Awards

"Witty, vivid, and very thought provoking, these interwoven narratives of the most sophisticated of primitive lusts start with a gay caveman who happens to have been around over fourteen thousand years....
Really, you've just got to read this!"
 — Samuel R. Delany

"Rebecca Ore pulls off an audacious experiment: using the raw language and deliberate focus on sexual encounters of 'slash' fiction to relate a series of linked episodes and moments of reflection from the stupendously long life of a gay male, from his earliest days as a mammoth-hunting caveman to around the present."
 — Faren Miller, *Locus,* June 2009

"Ah, but a true power chord is infinitely replenishable, given enough talent on the part of the author. And Rebecca Ore proves this to the max.... Vel is utterly believable—and believably strange—as a fusion of pre-modern, postmodern, and timeless attitudes and habits. A cousin to our species, yet not exactly in our direct lineage."
 —Paul Di Filippo *Asimov's Science Fiction,* March 2010

"*Centuries Ago and Very Fast*...has a kinetic energy and hard-to-define originality that held me captivated from first word to last. Profane—scandalous?—the book wraps stories around stories, combines the surreal with the mundane and every-day."
 —Jeff VanderMeer, *Locus Online,* February 11, 2010